DAY OF THE GUN

DAY OF THE GUN

WILLIAM R. COX

WHEELER
CHIVERS

This Large Print edition is published by Wheeler Publishing, Waterville, Maine, USA and by BBC Audiobooks Ltd, Bath, England.
Wheeler Publishing is an imprint of Thomson Gale, a part of The Thomson Corporation.
Wheeler is a trademark and used herein under license.

LIBRARY OF CONGRESS CATALOGING-IN-PUBLICATION DATA

Cox, William Robert, 1901–
   Day of the gun / by William R. Cox.
     p. cm. — (Wheeler Publishing large print western)
   ISBN-13: 978-1-59722-581-6 (pbk. : alk. paper)
   ISBN-10: 1-59722-581-9 (pbk. : alk. paper)
   1. Large type books. I. Title.
PS3553.O9466D39 2007
813'.54—dc22   2007016626

BRITISH LIBRARY CATALOGUING-IN-PUBLICATION DATA AVAILABLE

Published in 2007 in the U.S. by arrangement with
Golden West Literary Agency.
Published in 2007 in the U.K. by arrangement with
Golden West Literary Agency.

U.K. Hardcover: 978 1 405 64210 1 (Chivers Large Print)
U.K. Softcover: 978 1 405 64211 8 (Camden Large Print)

Printed in the United States of America on permanent paper
10 9 8 7 6 5 4 3 2 1

DAY OF THE GUN

PROLOGUE

It was growing late in the afternoon when the Captain of Rurales made polite farewells, saying that the Border and Ciudad Juarez and the El Paso del Norte were but a few miles northward and for him there was pressing business elsewhere. Daniel David Logan did not like it, but he made the best of it, there being eight of the Mexican police and only himself and Ambrose.

When the police had gone, Ambrose squinted at the sun, then at the irregular hills ahead and raised an eyebrow. "What you reckon?"

Logan said, "I reckon El Puma."

"I dunno any El Puma. Trouble, that I can smell." Ambrose was a former Ranger, a tall Texan, lanky, with a long, blond mustache, somewhat lugubrious in aspect, though not without humor. Logan had not been acquainted with him before this expedition to Mexico City. Indeed, Ambrose had been a late courier, arriving just prior to the conclusion of the secret and delicate confabulations which Logan had been conducting with certain officials of the Mexican government. Colonel Barty in El Paso seemed to set great store by Ambrose, trusting him with last moment trade secrets which had aided in the successful conclusion of the mission.

More than that the ex-Ranger was Barty's man, Logan did not know. They were journeying home, each with his own thoughts, each keeping his own counsel. Colonel Barty was always one for devious methods, representing the United States as Commissioner of Affairs in the Southwest, moving to perform his duties in mysterious ways, Logan thought, and paying none too well.

"There's a town ahead, Asienta. If you can call it a town," he told Ambrose, as they rode into the afternoon. "I've been there. But El Puma now, he's a thing to avoid. This is his country. He's a ten cent revolutionary."

"Bandit, you mean?"

"An odd sort," Logan said, remembering what he knew of El Puma. "All kinds of odd. Don't let him catch you alive."

"Bad as that, huh?"

"Real bad," Logan told him. "You know

we can't stand together if anything happens?"

"Sure. One of us gets back to the Colonel." Ambrose wiped his mustache with long
fingers, curling the ends. "That's why we
ain't carrying no papers."

"One of us gets back to report," agreed
Logan. "If we're caught, we don't talk. But
take my advice, kill yourself before giving
up. El Puma can make anybody talk."

It was then Logan saw the riders, skylined
for a moment, then vanishing into the
growth of pine and fir atop the highest hill.
He took out a folding spyglass and searched
the points of the compass. They were not
even bothering to conceal themselves. They
were all around, ex-vaqueros for the most
part, great horsemen and knowledgeable of
the terrain. He knew their kind; he knew
their weird, incomprehensible leader.

He said, "You'd better start trying to
forget me. Because right about now, we are
parting company."

"Yeah," said Ambrose. "I see what you
mean. Which way you figurin' on goin'?"

"Northwest, then around to the route to
El Paso. You'd best go southwest, try and
circle them. I've got the best horse. Let
them get closer, then we pull apart, fast. If I
can get in a shot, they'll chase me harder."

"You haven't anything on me when it comes to the long gun," argued Ambrose. "Lemme take the shot."

Before Logan could unlimber his rifle Ambrose had fired, in seemingly offhand fashion. The leader of the troop threw up his hands and fell from the saddle. The troop reacted as Logan had known they would, electing for vengeance, riding on an angle to cut off Ambrose from the rear. It looked as though the way northward might be clear for time enough for a run. He aimed for a clump of high brush, thinking he might keep them out of view for enough time to get a long lead.

He was going past the brush at a full gallop when four men came at him. Logan shot the leader with his rifle, letting the second swiftest come closer, firing again, dropping the horse and tumbling the rider.

Circling around, he had a view of the mountain and of Ambrose. A whirling reata swept over the shoulders of the Texan; he was thrown heavily from the saddle and lay still as they closed in on him. There would be no opportunity to kill himself even had he wished.

Logan reversed his direction and with the sun at his back, he charged the two Mexican riders. The surprise attack confused the pursuers, now the pursued. They split apart but not very far as Logan came in, firing once, then twice. Each was shot in the head.

Logan reined in the horse. It would be a straight run into Asienta now, he thought. He would have to think about Ambrose and wonder if El Puma would take him to that village, indeed, the only settlement in the area. The horse would not go much farther and there was this girl, Maria. . . .

The vaquero he had shot down by dropping the horse raised to his knees and fired pointblank. Logan drew and snapped his six-shooter. The man fell back.

But Logan's horse flinched and flagged.

It would be, he thought, wearily, a long, dusty walk to Asienta that evening. He turned his face in that direction and walked, carrying only his revolver, wearing the shell belt, everything else discarded.

CHAPTER ONE

Asienta was squalid and the darkness could not disguise the odor of pigs wallowing in the gutters. Daniel David Logan stumbled over a squealing runt and regretted the six inches of height which forced him to bend low to maintain the disguise of conical sombrero and enveloping serape. A sliver of lamplight came from the lone cantina. A woman laughed on a high, pleasurable note.

Well, Maria, the woman he'd enlisted, had furnished, for a price, the hat and the serape. Logan's feet hurt, but he had slept and he had been fed, this thrown in with the disguise, and now he must have a horse and he must do something about Ambrose, because, as he had imagined, they had brought Ambrose to the town and were dealing with him in the cantina.

This El Puma, real name Miguel de Santa Ferra, was a man of varied parts, Logan knew. He was a Mexican with connections above the border, about which Logan would like to know a lot more. He had some connections in Mexico City, also, but there were always crackpots who desired the overthrow of the government there. The United States at this time wanted no truck with them, it was for the status quo and in his way, Logan was working for the government at Washington, D.C.

It was, Logan repeated, necessary that Ambrose did not talk, because Colonel Barty had trusted his Texan with far too much inside knowledge. There was no question that El Puma could make him talk. The man did not live who would not babble under certain Yaqui treatment. The Asienta street narrowed under his feet and he could see the stable behind the cantina and the side window from which the light emanated. He crept along the adobe wall, his fingertips sensitive to its rough surface.

The window was larger than most in this country but without glass or wax paper, just a hole in the wall admitting insects and cool night air. There was the sound of jollity within, the tequila was flowing, the woman laughed again. Logan edged closer and surveyed the scene within the cantina.

El Puma was a dandy, wearing a velveteen bolero jacket, slashed bell bottom trousers

14

and a scarlet shirt open at the throat. His wide upper lip was pencilled by a black mustache, his eyes were wide-spaced and cruel and feral. Upon his lap was a female whose short skirt was racked up high above her plump knees. But no one was looking at Conchita, sister of Maria. All were staring across the room, laughing, mocking. There were eight of them, including the leader, so that Logan knew the others were out on the plains searching for him.

Tomas Gomez, spidery, menacing, was across the room, as was Gorda the Apache with his curved, razor-edged scalping knife. And Ambrose was there.

Logan started, staring at Ambrose. They had tied him with a reata, into a tight bundle. They had suspended him upside down from a butcher's hook in the ceiling beam. The lamps were all turned high so that the anguish of the Yanqui victim could be enjoyed without discrimination. The girl laughed again as El Puma teased her beneath the skirt.

Ambrose was already bleeding from small, crisscross cuts on his cheeks. His mouth was working, his straggly blonde mustache was like a caterpillar on a hot stove. There was a small brazier on the floor, directly beneath the former Ranger's skull. Sweat poured

15

down and his eyes were already beginning to craze as the heat reached his brainpan.

Logan placed the remaining five vaqueros in his mind, knowing they would be fascinated, unmoving for the next few moments. El Puma was asking questions about the reason for the presence of two Yanqui riders in what he referred to as his country. Ambrose was ready to talk, but could not, Logan thought.

A revolver shot would end it. He hesitated. Maria had slid up to him out of the shadows, and was tugging gently at him. He backed away from the window, crouching low, and whispered into her ear.

"You will go to the stable and bring me a horse. Thus, I shall make a run for my life. And it would be best if you drove the remaining horses out the rear door of the barn."

Creeping back toward the window, the Colt in his hand, he could hear El Puma plainer, now, mocking, asking.

"You are merely givin' pleasure to Gorda, y'know, my friend. To me it is nothin', really. Why not get comfy and tell us all about it, eh?" The astounding British accent of which El Puma was extremely proud, had been acquired when he was exposed to education at Oxford. His family had been wealthy

16

under a previous administration in Mexico. He continued, "You and your pal came down to spy upon me. Just tell me about it, be a friend."

Ambrose's voice was a hoarse, stubborn mumble. "That ain't true."

El Puma plucked a cigarro from his jacket. Tomas scratched a taper and held it to the end, which glowed to life. Logan sighed, wondering about the girl and if she could handle the horses before he was forced to kill the dangling Texan.

It was too bad about Ambrose. He had not learned that it was better to talk. Tell lies, tell anything rather than defy people like these.

The truth, in fact, was a tricky matter. The negotiations in Mexico City had been off the record. Indeed, Colonel Barty's position was in itself anomalous, since "Commissioner of Affairs" never did mean anything except what certain powers-that-be in Washington allowed at any given moment. The problem was that El Puma must know nothing of the errand just accomplished lest he use it to increase his forces against the government in Mexico or the government in the United States.

Ambrose knew too much. Maybe Barty had a good reason for divulging too much,

Logan had no way to measure that answer. Maybe Barty was somewhat of a fool, but Logan doubted this. Barty always had something held back; Barty had much influence in high circles. It was just that Ambrose had been unlucky and now it looked as though he would be dead.

El Puma's cigar was burning freely. He arose, depositing the girl on the floor, smiling. He approached the suspended figure of the Texan.

"It will now be necessary to remove your — ah — trousers, my friend. There are parts, you know, which are especially susceptible to fire. If you are, afterwards, no longer a man . . . bad show, what?"

They were stretching the ex-Ranger on the table. The girl was against the wall, highly interested. El Puma was talking; he enjoyed dramatics.

"It will be very painful. There is a certain odor that I deplore, y' know. Burning flesh. Burning hair. Very nasty. But you will talk. My, yes, how you will chat. All about the Texicans and what their plans are and how they intend to make a move against us."

They were working at Ambrose's belt. He came to life suddenly. Logan stared. The Ranger had been playing a bit of possum, at that. He was hand-fighting Gorda. Three of the others had to fling themselves into the action. They pressed him down on the table top.

El Puma was saying in unaltered tones, "And about our friends. Do they know about our friends? How much do they know? Simple questions, old boy. Must have the answers, y' know."

Logan steadied the revolver barrel on the sill of the window. Maria, he assumed, had failed. Gorda was at the belt holding up Ambrose's pants.

Noise broke out in the direction of the barn. Logan stepped back from the window, crouching a little, cursing beneath his breath, knowing Maria had somehow botched it. There was a small explosion, which might be a lamp blowing up. There was a loud scream, then, amazingly, the pounding of horses on the dirt.

They came toward him. Maria had turned them loose, but the quick blaze behind them showed their terrified silhouettes rushing through fear, directly toward the cantina. The barn, dry as tinder, would be fully enveloped in a moment. Logan took a step in that direction, then slammed back against the wall, blocked by the horses. Maria screamed again.

El Puma bellowed, "Manuel! Durango!

Hold the Yanqui! Quick, to the horses."

The window was on his right; Logan risked a look. Only the two guards were left, and the girl in a corner. It was made to order. He steadied the Colt and fired two quick shots inside the room, hoping the sound would be covered by the confusion. The two, Manuel and Durango, went down, headshot, making no noise about it. Logan went through the window.

He cut Ambrose's hands loose. There was a mask of dried blood on the ex-Ranger's face but he managed a grin and two words. "Hello, Dan'l."

"Get up from there and grab their guns," Logan said. He was watching the girl in the corner. When her hand came up with a gun in it, he shot her in the shoulder. "Naughty, naughty. C'mon, will you, Ambrose?"

"Just a little stiff," said Ambrose, staggering toward the door in Logan's wake. "That El Puma, he don't fool around much."

"You'll be completely stiff if we don't find a couple of horses in this stampede," Logan told him. "Damnedest women around here, for a small town."

He headed for the burning stable. Maria lay half in, half out of the wide door. In the starlight he saw there was a terrible wound in her head. He spun around and shoved at

Ambrose.

"There *were* a couple of unusual women. Try for the street. Maybe we can bushwhack us a horse or two."

Ambrose hobbled along as the two of them took a station at the edge of the cantina wall, their guns ready. The barn was now burning furiously and people were straggling from their adobe hovels, bleary-eyed and frightened. Voices rose, excited, shrill. The water supply was from cisterns, there would be no chance of saving the barn . . . indeed the village would be in dire danger in a few minutes.

Ambrose stamped his feet to restore circulation and observed, "Always heard you could head-shoot and get away with it. Most people are belt buckle shots."

"Time and circumstance," Logan told him. "Now it seems to me that Maria, the girl back yonder, had time to saddle up at least one horse. Maybe two. Her mistake was in lighting the damn lantern. Must have kicked it over. A shame, but there you have it. Keep your eye peeled for saddled horses."

"They'll be long gone to Texas."

"I know. Might as well follow, hadn't we?"

"Walk?" Ambrose was horrified. He was a man who wouldn't walk to the corner for the makin's if a horse was available.

Logan said, "There's more of El Puma's dandy little bunch around and about. I'd hate to be a sitting duck when they start looking."

Ambrose said, "Well, mebbe. We got a couple short guns. I took a belt along, which is stuffed with cartridges. If we do run into 'em, remind me to shoot myself before they hogtie me again. That fella made me plumb nervish, the way he was comin' at me when hell busted loose."

"He's a little beauty, all right. I wonder what he meant about his friends above the Border?"

"I wouldn't know. I wasn't listenin', much."

"Uh-huh," said Logan. Then he drew back into deeper shadow. "Hey! Look yonder."

Two riders were coming in. They were walking their horses, rifles at the ready. The blaze from the barn revealed that they had not been among those in the cantina with El Puma.

Logan said, "Simple, isn't it? Just lucky, that's all."

Shouting and movement amidst the crackling of flame filled the night with noise. The riders, puzzled, slowed down, looking right and left. In another moment they would be athwart of the spot where the two Americanos waited.

"How about the one on the left?" Logan asked.

"You take him."

Logan fired offhand. Ambrose took his time aiming. The rider on the left went over backwards, hit in the skull. The one on the right sagged like a sack half full of beans. Ambrose seized the reins of the nearest horse. There was a yell and El Puma's voice screamed an order in Spanish.

Logan said, "Take it away, Ambrose. Go that way." He pointed a finger. "See you in El Paso."

He made a flying mount and spurred in the opposite direction from that which Ambrose took. A man aimed a rifle at him and he shot above the barrel, between the eyes. It was time to run and he lay on the horse's neck, kicking at the ribs. El Puma and a gaggle of bodyguards came in sight and he emptied his remaining chambers.

The horse seemed a good one. Bullets fanned his ears, but he made it east to the edge of the town and then swung north. There was a broad trail and he set sail for the Rio Grande with all possible speed.

Chapter Two

The gaming room in the Hotel El Paso del Norte was fashionable. Well dressed men and well upholstered women grouped about the tables. The bar was mahogany, polished as high as the back mirror. Negro and Mexicano boys bustled with trays of food and drink. Daniel David Logan, in newly purchased dark jacket, striped trousers, white shirt, string tie and hand-sewn boots stood at the roulette wheel and listened for a telltale click, betting lightly, in his fashion, more interested in feminine pulchritude than gaming.

Ambrose put a hand on his arm. "Hi, Dan'l."

"Ambrose," said Logan. "How stands the watch?"

"He wants to see you."

"He's been taking his time."

"Well, you know. Hadda get word from headquarters."

"Big business."

"He wants to see you now." Ambrose bore scars which made his face older, somewhat sinister. Gorda had carved muscles which had not repaired. The Texan wore range clothing, a loose vest. His gun was tied low and he seldom removed his hat. He was a man for outdoors and a horse, Logan thought, maybe not brilliant, a faithful, steady, dependable man.

"I'll be there."

"See you," said Ambrose, turning away, stepping carefully in his high-heeled riding boots. He went out of the gaming place and onto the streets of El Paso.

It was not so long ago, Logan ruminated, that El Paso was a part of Mexico. Then the town had been known as "Franklin" until 1859. The Federals had occupied it, including Fort Bliss, during the war and had commanded the pass to the north.

The railroads had come after the war and then the town had become a city. John Wesley Hardin was from hereabouts and Logan remembered crossing pistols, to no decision, with that worthy in Silver. A no-good kid, Hardin, he thought, not really gun quick, but cold-blooded when certain of his victim. There were a lot of them on the frontier, bullies without redeeming characteristics.

The frontier? The world, he added, remembering West Point and the reason he had not finished there.

Silver City, West Point, each recurred to him when he was in this retrospective mood which made him so restless and unhappy.

He walked down Magoffin Street remembering the home place where his father had died and everything had gone out of New Mexico so far as Daniel Logan was concerned. There was a mine, too, worked out, disused, forgotten. Did the grama grass still grow in the meadows?

Ed Badger should be prosperous by now. Ed had been a good friend of the Logans. And his daughter, Susan Badger . . . well, forget about Susan. It's been a long time, you've learned about women, forget hell out of Susan.

He wondered if the house, so well constructed, had fallen in by now. It didn't matter, he persisted. It was another time, another young Daniel, nothing could bring back the happiness of innocence. Nothing could restore the way he had felt about Susan, his first romance. Forget her, he repeated, you've done a good job, stick to it.

He only thought of her now in this mood. He had grown to eschew sentimentality of all sorts. Since his dismissal from the Point he had scorned discipline, excepting when self-imposed. He did not yet know his destiny, but he knew how to exist, he told himself. Gambling, women, good liquor and plenty of excitement, these were the elements in which he moved at his best. He had amazingly good reflexes and the swiftest hands. In a country of the short gun he was easily one of the kings.

Working undercover for various Cattlemen's Associations, the United States Government, the Pinkertons was all part of the game. The rewards were meager but he was sometimes a lucky gambler. When good fortune ran out he would go back to work, as of now.

He was coming to Barty's house. It stood out in the neighborhood, two stories high. It had been built by a Spanish merchant who couldn't buck the interests brought in by the railroads and the ineffable Colonel had got it for the proverbial song. Barty was always lucky, Logan thought. Since he had proclaimed himself "colonel" during a Comanche skirmish against frightened militia which had somehow survived, he had gone once to Congress and twice to the State Legislature. He had the proper connections to get himself made Commissioner of Affairs, a title meaning nothing on the surface but relating to every kind of underground activity in Texas, Arizona and New Mexico. What with rails, mining, ever-increasing cattle interests and the constant intrigue between the country to the south and the

American Southwest, Barty was a busy man.

The house was shuttered, but light crept beneath a shade in the rear. Logan once again checked his backtrack, then walked to a side door and knocked in a certain manner.

From within a voice asked, "Logan?"

"It's not my brother." These small byplays were a bore, a childish game.

Ambrose opened the door. The light struck on his scarred face. He was solemn, one hand on his gun, checking to make certain it was indeed Logan. "Come in, Dan'l."

The room was furnished as an office, with one heavy door leading to the rest of the house, a small bookcase containing volumes of records and legal tomes, a Spanish desk, very heavy and ornate, hangings on each wall to deaden sound, a thick carpet. Behind the desk sat Colonel Slidell Barty, whiskers and all, wearing a diamond ring, a flowered silk vest, a ruffled shirt. At his plump hand was an ugly over-and-under derringer. On his lips was a warm smile.

"Howdy, Daniel. Good to see you again."

"Colonel Barty." Logan had never liked the man. His eyes were amber, catlike. His hair was long and wavy and what could be seen of his mouth was sensual, petulant despite the ever present smile.

"Sit down, have a cigar." The box was of polished wood, the tobacco warm and redolent of spice.

Logan sat on a straight chair. Ambrose leaned against the wall, silent.

Barty said, "Washington was right pleased with your little trip down south."

"Well, I'm not pleased with Washington, D. C.," said Logan. "It doesn't pay enough."

"Only so much can be allowed." But Barty's amber colored eyes became sleepy, like a cat's. "I surmise you'd go to work again, right now."

"I need the money. I'm for sale," Logan told him.

"You mean for hire."

"Easy words. When you put it on the line, you're for sale. They shoot at you. It's for keeps."

"You got a point, there," Barty said, chuckling. "Never thought of it thataway. You got a point."

"And next time, the expenses must be a bit more generous. I almost didn't have enough to bribe a broke Mexican girl this trip."

"You're not goin' that far, this time. Just up country a ways, in fact. New Mexico."

"I see. New Mexico." Logan puffed on the

cigar. "Something to do with wetbacks."

"You know about that." Barty's voice softened, his smile widened. "You heard El Puma talkin' about it."

Logan did not correct the Colonel. He refrained from looking at Ambrose. Two and two usually equaled four, and to disillusion these two men would be stupid.

Barty picked a sheet of paper from a folder and said, "You from New Mexico . . . right?"

"New York," said Logan.

"You was born in New York. But you was taken to New Mexico when a child," Barty said. "Your papa was an engineer, took up minin', gave you an education at home. You all had a ranch near Bailey, in the Silver City country, twixt there and Santa Rita . . . right?"

"You're telling it," said Logan, stifling annoyance.

"It's all here, in your West Point record. You got yourself fired from West Point. That's the year your papa died of the fever and your ma, too. Lots of people died of the fever that year."

"Lots of people," agreed Logan, closing his eyes, managing to control himself.

"The mine petered out. Your pa had some cattle. You sold the stock, but you never sold the property. It's up for taxes about now, did you know that?"

"I know."

"You began driftin'. Picked up with Luke Short, gambled a lot. Shot a few folk, but they needed it, mainly."

"They needed it always," Logan said harshly. "And that part isn't in any West Point record."

"Washington, D.C. has to know these things," said Barty. "You marshaled a couple towns . . . What ever did happen with you and John Wesley Hardin?"

"He's mainly scared," said Logan. "I let him be that way."

"Interestin'," said Barty. "Trigger-happy and therefore some scared. John Wesley's right bright, though."

"It wasn't noticeable," Logan said.

Barty returned to his paper. "Says here that you're a real quick gun. No nerves. Accurate. People in Washington, D.C. think highly of you."

"They liked Wild Bill, too. And Buffalo Bill. Back there they like all us big western shooters."

"No use to be sarcastic," said Barty. "They like you. I like you. And we got a problem in Bailey, New Mexico, and that's your home country."

"I would like to pay taxes on the ranch,"

31

Logan admitted to Barty and to himself. He had not been certain that he cared, now he knew.

"We want you to do that." Barty paused, then said, "You know about Bailey?"

"It's grown some, I hear."

"It's grown ridiculous. Man from New York come in there, name of Simon Maxton. Runs things, he does."

"Mining?"

"Nope."

"Cattle?"

"Some. Includin' wetback trade. Not as much as will be, some day."

"Then what is it that makes Bailey so big?"

"Drugs."

"Drugs? You mean — opium, heroin?"

"And cocaine," said Barty. "From Europe, from China. It gets to Bailey. It goes to Maxton. Then it is shipped out all over the country. Millions of dollars." The cat-eyes shone, then were hooded by heavy lids. "Got to be stopped, Logan."

"What's the connection between drugs and El Puma?" Logan was guessing again, but he was fairly certain of his ground. "How come he raids if he's in traffic?"

"Since when has he raided?"

Logan thought a moment. "It has been several months, hasn't it?"

"Almost a year."

"All right," said Logan. "But I'll want enough money to operate, this time. And to pay my taxes. Free and clear. Because I don't really want to go back to New Mexico, Colonel."

"You always want money."

"I'm always putting my neck in a noose, or sticking my head in front of a gun muzzle."

"I'll tell you," Barty said, and now he did look toward Ambrose for an instant, then back to Logan, then to a tin box which he produced as though by sleight of hand. "I want you to go to Bailey and pay your taxes. Truly. I want you to pretend to search for cattle to stock the ranch. . . . Rockin' Chair, ain't it?"

"Rocking Chair," said Logan. He had not called its name aloud in years. "That's right, Rocking Chair."

"Washington, D.C. wants that drug business stopped. Furthermore, Logan, I want some special information."

"You?"

"Me, personally. I got property up around Bailey, around Silver. I got a notion to ranch it there, some day. I don't want no Simon Maxtons around. Is that plain?"

"You want him dead."

33

"Or long gone." Barty opened the box and began removing greenbacks. "This here is my personal money. I got to, you know, watch gov'ment money. With my own I'm different. I pay off."

"You must own a lot of property up there."

"You just get rid of Maxton. These here will take care of expenses." He shoved two wads of the cash across the desk. "You put it out that you got money and Maxton will come after you. He's got a big nose for cash. He runs Bailey, all the way, top to bottom. He makes deals with the locals, like Mel Carraway, other folk, but he's the boss, you better remember."

"Mel Carraway of Lazy Dog Ranch?"

"The same."

"I grew up with him."

"Carraway's goin' to marry a gal name of Susan Badger," Barty said. "Her old man owns the only other spread of any size."

"Cross B," said Logan mechanically. Talking with Barty was like playing poker, you had to watch every moment. "Ed Badger is quite a man."

"He's an old drunk," said Barty bluntly.

"You must be out of your mind!"

"Ed Badger is an old drunk. I dunno why, I dunno a hell of a lot of things I want you to find out. But I do know Ed Badger's no

34

force up there. Carraway is kind of a big, dumb fella but if Maxton's callin' the turns, could be Carraway's a problem. I want it cleaned up. I want my property protected. Washington, D.C. wants the traffic in drugs to be busted. Here is enough money to pay off your taxes and buy some stock. Is it a deal?"

"It's generous," said Logan slowly. "What's the catch, Colonel?"

"Same old story. You just sold your gun again."

Ambrose shifted against the wall. He looked at Logan, shrugged, turned away. A fly buzzed around the ceiling, roosted on the top of a picture of George Washington.

Logan said, "Okay. It's a deal."

"Leave in the morning?" Barty asked.

"Soon as I can buy a horse and my gear."

"Right," said Barty. "Pick up the marbles."

Logan took an empty money belt from his pocket and neatly stacked the cash therein. Barty allowed himself a rare grin, watching.

"You a real cutter, Logan. You really are. You always ready."

"Better to be asked and ready," said Logan. He lifted a hand. "See you boys later."

Ambrose sat on the chair vacated by Logan. For a moment there was only the sound of the buzzing fly and the breathing of the two men.

Then the Colonel said, "You see how it is?"

"I see."

"Just plain bad damn luck, El Puma catchin' you thataway. Logan's awful smart. He adds up, real good."

"El Puma don't know about you and me."

"Of course he don't. Would he be torturin' you if he knew? Make sense, Ambrose. Don't make me do all the thinkin'."

"I never was much at thinkin'." Ambrose dropped his chin into a fist. "I don't like this, somehow."

"You don't have to like it."

"Ain't we got enough? Can't we just leave it go?"

Barty sighed. His voice became very low and more than ever rich with the intonation of the deep south. "Have I got to go through it all again? You remember who we are, Ambrose? You remember Papa?"

"I don't want to remember Papa."

"You remember Claiburn? Up the river in Alabama? The plantation? The slaves?"

"I remember." Ambrose's eyes were moist.

"Papa always claimed he was overseer. You know what he was, common laborer. No better than the nigras. Oh, he thought he

36

was better. But even the nigras knew. Who did we play with in the yard?"

"The nigras," whispered Ambrose. "White folks called us pore trash."

"We got away," Barty reminded him. "We come here. We made pretty good here, brother, you and me. We gonna make it better. We gonna be rich and we gonna be somebody. Rich first, because it's necessary. But important is the thing. We gonna be important. And no Simon Maxton is goin' to cross us and get away with it."

"I could handle it, honest I could."

"I don't want you handlin' it. People don't know it, but you're my brother. I want you clean. When the time comes, I want you with me, Ambrose, you unnastand? Clean!"

"How clean?" There was bitterness in the tone of his voice. "You know I got to do what must be."

"That'll be all right. You'll be workin' for me. For Washington, D.C."

"Logan yanked me outa that cantina when it was bad. He coulda killed me and run. He got me out. I like Logan."

"I like Logan, too."

"I wish there was some other way."

"Logan will have to kill Maxton. By then, he'll know too much. Logan is too smart, that's the whole trouble. I wish it wasn't that way, I could use Logan. He just ain't one that can be used, is all."

"Yeah, that's for true." Ambrose sighed, "You know the worst thing of all about it?"

"What?"

"I can't outdraw Logan in a thousand years," said Ambrose sadly. "I'll have to backshoot the sonofabitch."

CHAPTER THREE

The road wound through broken, hilly country with juniper, pinon and oak on both sides, mainly pinon. Daniel Logan remembered the boyhood hunt for the pinon nuts with Mel Carraway and stupid Santos Barela, the fat boy, and Susan Badger, the tomboy. The road to Silver was ahead and he would turn off for Bailey soon. He pulled up, swept the black horse from the trail and rode to the top of a hill, surrounded by the Cook Mountains, the Mogollons in view, all the Mimbrenos country around him.

It had been a hard country when his parents had brought him to New Mexico. The land taken up by the Logans was not the worst nor was it the best. As time developed the layout, water proved its best advantage. The Carraway ranch to the east and the Badger spread to the west were much larger and better situated, but the Logans had the water and all agreed to share and share on roundups and other disputatious matters. Nothing had been too hard to take when Daniel went to West Point.

He dismounted and led the black horse beneath a spreading pinon. Nostalgia, he thought, was something to face up to, then put aside. If he divested himself of sentimentality now, he could face them all later on, as he would have to face them, without weakness. It was not far from here to the place where he had first kissed Susan Badger, for instance.

Much more occurred thereafter. It was not proper, it was against all teaching, it was primal. They had been shaken by it but unafraid. When he became an officer in the Army of the United States they would marry and begin life on their own. Not that the families had disapproved. Quite the contrary, it was a matter of great happiness to the Logans and the Badgers.

Then, in his third year, the world had collapsed. The cholera came to the Apaches and was borne into the countryside and Mrs. Badger and both Logans were wiped out. They never knew that Daniel David had been discharged from the Academy that very week for disobedience, insubordination and striking an enlisted man.

When he had come home his parents were buried, Ed Badger was gone on a trip to forget and Susan was in a girl's school in Virginia. Santos Barela was a town loafer around Silver City. Mel Carraway was working his ranch, his own parents wiped out in the plague. Bailey was growing, there were eighty people clustered there around the store and the saloon. Billy the Kid was acquiring notoriety.

Now Billy was mouldering in his grave these two years and Pat Garrett was doing a lot of talking but was no longer in New Mexico. And Susan was engaged to be married to Mel Carraway.

Bailey was a big town, no one quite knew how or why. Daniel David Logan was returning as an undercover agent for Colonel Barty and the Government which had rejected him as an officer and a gentleman but accepted him as a spy and a sort of detective. He sat upon the hilltop and remembered his parents, whom he had loved. He remembered Susan whom he had probably not loved enough.

He had never seen Susan Badger from the time he left for the east until now. In his grief and disappointment and rage, he had left the ranch within a week. He had not sold it, he could not. But he had fled from the country which held so much tragedy, suffering with his own trouble at the Point. All the charges had been true: he had disobeyed a pompous command given him by a cadet he had beaten for the boxing team; he had refused to apologize for the act; he had knocked down a stable sergeant who was abusing his horse. It did not make his failure to adhere to the system any easier to know that, given the opportunity, he would have acted precisely in the same way again and again.

Now he knew he could not really go back home, he was just doing a job. He pushed all the tendrils of sentiment firmly away. He ground out the cigarette, remounted the black horse and rode over the hill toward the town of Bailey.

The town was traditional, it was laid out with the wide, unpaved main stem, across which at right angles were numbered streets where the inhabitants dwelt. There was little paint but a strong smell of resin from green lumber. The hotel was called MAXTON HOUSE. He tied up at the rail and swung around, surveying the scene.

Across from the hotel was a big saloon

with gimcrack stuck across its face. This was MAXTON'S PALACE. Next door to the hotel, with a breezeway connection linking the two buildings, was a honky tonk dance hall which even now, in the afternoon, emitted raucous sounds. This was MAXTON HALL.

There were other saloons and Dinty Magin's undertaking parlor and a general store and a livery stable and a small catchall shop with a sign saying JEWELRY AND NOTIONS and a bake shop and a Wells Fargo office with a telegraph wire running from it to a peeled pole in its rear. However, in the main Colonel Barty had certainly been correct, this was Maxton's town.

Logan stripped his bedroll from behind the saddle and started across the walk. Behind him a harsh voice demanded, "Stop right where y'are, please, stranger."

Logan said, "Well, howdy do," and turned.

A fat, swarthy man in a dirty shirt, loose vest and baggy pants tucked into town boots was staring at him, hand on a long-barreled Buntline Special which was dangling in a beaded holster. His eyes were bloodshot and he seemed to be suffering from a long bout with John Barleycorn. He wore a drooping black mustache and a belligerent expression on vacuous features. A star was pinned to his vest.

"Dan Logan?" asked the apparition weakly. "It's you?"

"You mean they let you play marshal in this burg?" demanded Logan. "Santos Barela, peace officer? Have they gone altogether loco?"

"Now, Dan," complained the marshal. "Don't you start that. What you doin' home, anyhow?"

"Came to plague all fat men," said Logan cheerfully.

"There you go," said Santos. "Startin' up on me. You can't do that no more. I'm the law here."

"Why sure. I understand," Logan said. He tossed his bundle onto the verandah of the hotel. "You have dignity these days. Lost your accent and everything."

"I got a place here in Bailey. You'll soon find out," said Barela.

"I'll bet," Logan said. "Say, you have a spot on your shirt there. See?"

He reached out and when Santos dropped his chin in pure reaction, Logan's finger snapped up under the marshal's nose in the old, timeless schoolboy trick that he had practiced hundreds of times in years gone by. Barela yowled.

"Same old Santos," Logan said. "You

haven't changed a bit, really. Now what was it you wanted to see me about?"

"I see everybody comes into this town," yammered the marshal. "I got a job to do, Dan Logan, you unnastand that. You can't mess with the law."

"Santos Barela, boy marshal. Did you get elected, old friend? Or were you appointed?"

"You'll larn, soon enough." There was spite in the strange, whining voice which should have been tinted with Spanish intonation and was not, since its owner had tried to avoid his compatriots from school days. "Things ain't like they was around here."

"I believe you." Logan tried to sound solemnly impressed but did not succeed very well. "Who's the mayor of this new and prosperous community?"

"Ain't got one. Never was one. Ain't incorporated. Or whatever."

Logan forced his eyes wide open in assumed awe. "Then you're the only law in Bailey?"

"That's about the size of it." Santos seemed reassured. "What you goin' to do, open the old place?"

"That's right," said Logan. "Made a few dollars, thought I'd come home."

"This ain't rightly your home," Santos

44

said, scowling. "Silver was more home when you left."

"Right again. But this is closer now, isn't it?"

"It ain't the same," Barela repeated.

"It's brand new."

"That ain't what I mean."

"And you're the law."

"That ain't it zactly, neither." The marshal was over his depth. The stupid fat boy had become a stupid fat man.

Down the street two men erupted from one of the smaller drinking establishments, crouched, bandy legged, stalking. One, by his garb, was a town citizen. The other was a lanky cowboy. They came together, voices sharply accusing, fell apart. The city man drew a knife.

The cowboy moved, slapped, knocked the shining blade away. The opponent tried to run. The cowboy hit him behind the neck, drove him into the dust.

"The majesty of the law," Logan murmured.

Barela said, "That there cowboy is Paul Crown. He works for Mel. He's a gun. He hates tinhorns somethin' awful. Now I'll have trouble straightenin' out another one of his thangs."

"How much do they pay you, Santos?"

"Two hundred and a dollar for every prisoner," said the marshal proudly. "Maxton pays good, I'll remark." Then he looked over his shoulder, up and down the street, his tongue coming out to lick at his mustache, his hand shaking. "I mean the town. I mean Bailey pays good."

"Yes. I see what you mean."

"Well, I got to go. Paul will kill that tinhorn if I don't talk to him."

The fat man waddled toward the cloud of dust in which the combatants struggled, the one to arise, the other to get his boot in a sore spot. Then the gambler rolled over twice and produced a derringer from his sleeve. There were two shots, quick and snapping, like firecrackers during a celebration. Logan leaped to the porch, flattening himself against the wall.

The gambler lay still. The cowboy blew through the barrel of his revolver, slipped two cartridges into place, turned around and saw Barela hiding behind a wagon.

"Cuss you, Santos, whyn't you get here in time to stop this?" called the killer in a high, nasal twang. "This here's the second crooked jackleg I've had to kill for you."

Dinty Magin came out of his shop and approached the hotel. He looked no different from the day Dan had last seen him; he wore the same hard hat and low heels and Levis flecked with sawdust. A gold collar button held his white shirt in place around his skinny neck, his blue eyes, wide-spaced showed no surprise.

"That you, Daniel?"

"What's left of me." He shook hands with the old cabinet maker. "Nice to see you again."

Down the street the gambler had drawn up his knees and was keening his death song. Barela gingerly accepted Crown's proffered revolver.

Magin said, "They ask for it, then when they're gutshot they cry themselves into hell."

"The cowboy makes real sure, doesn't he?"

"And quick," said Magin. "Brings me a lot of trade, Crown does. Then old Mel pays his fine and he's back to the Lazy Dog for awhile. Outa sight, outa mind."

"Mel's branched out some, hasn't he?"

"You heard?"

"I heard."

"Sure you did. Heard your place was goin' for taxes, too, didn't you?"

"Tomorrow's the deadline," said Logan. "You know where I can buy some good stock?"

Magin shook his head. "Hell of a time to come home, ain't it?"

"Maybe there'll never be a good time."

"Well, your gal is marryin' Mel. Ed Badger's drinkin' hisself to the grave. Simon Maxton's runnin' just about everything in sight."

"I'll want to know more about it, Dinty."

"Yeah. Right now I better pick up my corpus before he goes all the way and stiffens up on me." Magin went to the scene of the violence.

Logan went into the hotel. The lobby was small and dark, but a wide stairway led to rooms above and the place seemed clean enough. He put his bedroll on the desk and touched a hand bell. A young Mexican boy came from behind a curtain, rubbing his eyes.

"Si, senor. A room, maybe?"

Logan signed the register and handed over a four bit piece. "The best you have and put my things in it. I'll be back when I get here. Okay?"

"Okay, senor. I am Pedro." The boy had a nice grin. "I take care of you, senor."

Logan went back outdoors. The cowboy and Balera came abreast of the hotel, strolling toward the marshal's office down the street. He could hear Crown talking in his high, carrying voice.

"He was dealin' like I was a country boy. Truth to tell, I am a country boy, Santos, you know that. But I got smartened up in towns. So I tells this pimp and he comes back at me and we tangle and out into the street we go. Then he comes at me with this hidey gun. You know I can't stand tinhorns with no hidey guns. I do wish he'd stop yellin' like that. Upsets people."

As if on cue, the prone gambler was silent. Logan walked down to where he lay. A young man came with a black bag, the town physician. Magin had two of his carpenters waiting now, a shutter-like stretcher between them. The young doctor winced when he saw the holes made by two .45 slugs. The gambler was sucking for breath now, agony turning him fish belly white.

Magin said, "He may live awhile. That's Doc Sutton, he gives him a big shot of morphine. Better he should let 'em go quick. They double up before they go, usually about four A.M., and I got a hell of a time with 'em."

The stretcher bearers, who were Teutonic and muscular, picked up the dying man at Dr. Sutton's behest and placed him as best they could on the wooden shutter. They picked up the burden and started for Magin's shop with the medical man walking alongside, his sideburns quivering. Logan and Dinty followed.

They went to the side of a long, low building and through a door. The room was indeed small, but the bed was covered with a clean blanket. The gambler moaned as they moved him. Dr. Sutton was a pale young man, long-faced, and his whiskers were a soft, brown fur. He had an annoying habit of sucking at his cheeks, through nervousness, Logan thought.

A woman wrapped in a shawl came hastily into the room and went to the side of the bed. Her voice was hoarse with the whiskey she had consumed over the frontier years. "Can't you even take off his boots?"

She wore a beaded short dress beneath the Mexican shawl. Her legs were encased in tights of some cotton material; they were slightly lumpy and scarred. Her body was shapely enough, even voluptuous. Dr. Sutton promptly ceased making mouth noises and leaped to the shiny black boots of the victim, mumbling, "I'm sorry, Rose. We just brought him in, you know. I'm sorry."

The woman continued to look down at the white face. She looked worse than sad, Logan thought. She looked partly lost and partly bemused, as though no deep emotion was left to her. She reached out a soiled finger and touched the gambler's mouth. "He's still alive."

"I gave him something," said Sutton with importance.

"You would," she said. "The poor bastard. He wasn't much, but he was what I wound up with."

Dinty Magin said, "I'll bury him for you, Rose."

"You always do." She never took her eyes from the waxen face. "He left me a few dollars. They're yours for a decent box and some flowers."

Magin began to speak, desisted. Logan walked away, leaned against the wall. The doctor got off the second boot and put them on the floor at the side of the cot. The woman bent and picked them up.

"New," she explained. "I gave 'em to him. Some cowboy will pay ten bucks for 'em, maybe." She turned away and moved to the door, pausing to give Logan a sharp look. Then she lifted one shoulder, as if realizing he was not the sort to do business with her, and went out into the street.

Logan watched her go into the dance hall. Magin was peering over his shoulder.

Magin said, "Keeps her head up pretty good for what she's come to."

"She looks familiar."

"Went to school with you. Rose Maguire. Father was foreman over to Dressen's, you know, the copper mine."

"Oh, yes, the wildcatter. Santa Rita drove them out of business."

"Maguire got hisself killed in the ruckus. Missus died in the plague. Rose went to work in Silver, then when Maxton come in, she was his gal for awhile. He wears 'em out fast. Drugs, some people say."

"Drugs?"

"Yeah, Cocaine. They sniff it up their nose." Magin shook his head. "They tried to get it from Doc, here, when they run low. Doc like to get kilt when he wouldn't do it."

Sutton said, "My oath prevents me from contributing to any such illegal business."

"But you're mighty hot after Rose," Magin thrust at him, dropping each word with intent.

The pale young man flushed to his whisker roots. "I feel for her."

"Yeah. You want the decent trade around here, you better get unfeelin' about whores like Rose," said Magin. "People talk."

"It's nobody's business but mine!"

Magin turned to Logan. "Hear him? The only doc around, he's feelin' his oats."

Logan said, "Sometimes you talk too much, Dinty."

"You bet I do. I'm the only one in town dares to talk about some things." Magin winked. "They need me to bury their dead, so they don't interfere."

"And you're getting rich," said the doctor bitterly. "You play on any side that pays money."

"And I live," agreed Magin. "You want trouble, Doc, you folley Dan'l around. He's a great one for trouble, allus was. He got into trouble at the West Point. He is one for always bein' in trouble."

Logan said, "Just want to buy some cows and settle down. No trouble at all."

"Mebbe we better go have a drink," suggested Magin. He jerked a thumb at the prone gambler. "He won't die 'til about three, four in the mornin'. They never do. Doc likes to stay with 'em, but I can tell you when they'll go."

Sutton said, "It's the decent thing to stay with a dying man."

"Sure," said Magin. "You stay. Comin', Daniel?"

"I'll join you in a moment," Logan told him. When the door had closed he went and stood at the foot of the cot with the young doctor.

"You're new here, aren't you?"

"I came here sixth months ago." Sutton spread his long, thin hands. "This is the tenth violent death."

"You mean by gunshot?"

"Not by any means. Four girls have committed suicide. There was one lynching. One knifing, very messy. The other three were gunshot."

"It's the suicides that bother you," suggested Logan.

"You're very perceptive." The hands wound around each other. "I'm not used to seeing women abused."

"Abused?"

"They do not kill themselves because they are happy, or well cared for," Sutton said. "Maxton is a brute. The men around him are brutes."

"Doesn't anyone stand up to Maxton?"

"Not a soul."

"What about Ed Badger?"

"He stands up to bars. More often he sits down in his own place and does his drinking."

"He was a good man."

"He may have been." Sutton sucked at his cheeks.

"Rose Maguire was a decent girl. Black Irish, we called her, for fun. She didn't even recognize me, just now."

"She wouldn't want you to know, perhaps."

"Could be."

"She is very emotional. Represses herself, but it's there, mainly despair, frustration. Ford was — well, he was her pimp. He treated her well."

"Does Rose take drugs?"

Sutton stared sharply at him. "What do you mean? They all take drugs."

"Her eyes. They weren't dilated. Her hands were steady. She seemed normal."

"You know these things." Sutton sighed. "I can't tell you about Rose. But I can tell you drug traffic in Bailey is big business. More and more addicts drift in. They hear about it, they come from everywhere. I think Maxton sends word to New York, Chicago, the big centers."

"This Maxton. He sounds like a bad customer."

"If you remain here, sir, you'll learn about him."

"Oh, I come from around here," said Logan. "I can take care of myself. Just trying to get the situation clear in my mind."

"The situation is that everyone walks a chalk line measured out by Simon Maxton."

"People walk a narrow path everywhere in

the world," Logan said. "Either one they drew out for themselves, or one they are forced to walk by others. It's a rough old place, the world. Good evening, sir." He went out of the little hospital room.

Dr. Sutton locked the door, then went to the side of the wounded man. There was motion beneath the blanket, the man called Ford groaned on an ascending note which wound up in a scream, his eyes opening, staring at the medico.

"You got to help me, Doc, you got to. I know I'm done for, you got to finish me."

Sutton said, "Take it easy, Ford."

"You got to. You got to." The scream was full-throated now, filling the corners of the small room. Sutton went to his bag. He was sweating. He took out cotton batten, separated it with damp hands. Ford was keening on a single note, his hands across the bandage on his belly. Nothing in the world hurt so much as punctured guts, Sutton thought, pouring chloroform on the cotton.

There was a knock on the door, a timid scratch. Sutton ignored it, going back to the bed, placing the odoriferous mass over the mouth and nostrils of Ford, whispering, "Good-bye, gambling man. Good-bye, joker. Rose won't need you now. Rose never did need you."

The tiny knock was repeated. Sutton left the cotton across Ford's face, lifting the curtain of the single narrow window, then unlocking the door, stepping back. Rose came quickly into the room, was assailed by the reeking smell, stared, knowing, at the man on the cot, then at Sutton.

The doctor said, "He asked for it."

She coughed, dashed a hand across her face as if wiping at cobwebs. "I believe you."

"It hurts, dying that way."

"I believe it." She was humble, looking at him, now, her penciled eyebrows raised. "What about me?"

He moved meticulously, lifting the chloroform mask, feeling the pulse of the man on the cot, nodding, then wrapping the cotton in a towel and shoving it far down into his bag, then producing a small vial of white powder and a tiny measuring spoon. He dusted a careful amount of cocaine upon the flat, shallow spoon and extended it to the woman.

She took it with equal care and gravity. She closed one nostril with a forefinger and sniffed. Then she did the same on the other side of her nose, closing her eyes, waiting patiently for the drug to take effect. He replaced the vial and the spoon and snapped the bag shut.

She asked, "Is he dead?"

"He's dead."

"He had his good points." Real color was returning to her cheeks. She dismissed Ford with a wave of the hand. "Daniel David Logan. What about him?"

"Magin says he is trouble."

"Magin's a fool in many ways," she said. "Did Barty send Daniel here or didn't he?"

"I don't know," he answered dully, avoiding her eyes.

"You've lost touch with El Paso?"

"Donovan was killed last week. By a man named Ambrose. It was a shootout."

"I see." She looked stronger now, her eyes had come alive. "Logan . . . I don't know. He was Susan's boy, long ago. Then he went to school."

"He speaks like an educated man."

"He's educated. And bitter. Losing his folks did something to him."

"He thinks you didn't recognize him."

"Good. I want to be sure of him before he thinks I'm any better than a lost cause." She sneered at Sutton. "If I am. Any more."

"You are." He gritted his teeth, his cheeks sucked in. "Nobody would know it, but you are."

"If Logan would come in with a fast gun. Ed Badger taught him, he's fast, all right."

She sighed. "Simon and those behind him are too smart, I reckon. Too mean, too bad. Maybe we need a lot of men with guns."

"We can't get them. We're isolated. I can't get through to anyone in authority. Donovan got killed trying."

She said, "I know . . . I know. Simon thinks he has it made, but something's wrong, some place."

"Has he been bothering you?"

"Simon?" She laughed. "He can't understand me. Never saw anyone kick the habit like I'm supposed to have done. Can't understand why I do my job without complaining. Can't understand why I'm not dead."

"The cowardly bastard."

"No, not a coward," she said. "He's the kid who picks wings off flies and dips 'em in the inkwell. But he'll fight at recess, too, that kind. Don't buy him for scared, Doc. He's the most dangerous around. It takes guts to be as dangerous as Simon Maxton."

"I guess you're right."

"Some things even someone like me has got to learn. But you're all right. You're not a western man, lots of things you don't understand, yet. But you're clever enough." She waved a hand. "We might not live through it, but it won't be for not trying.

And maybe we can get Logan with us."

"I'm not clever," he protested. "If I were, I could do something about you."

She regarded him with detachment. "When you came here, I was Maxton's gal. And I was hooked. A hooked hooker, Doc. A gone goose."

"No, not gone."

"You saw him ditch me. You saw me take up with Ford. You took interest in me."

"You were sick."

"Anyway, here I am. Only slightly hooked. Taperin' off on the stuff. Ford's dead." She indicated the corpse across the room with no more interest than if it had been a bundle of straw. "I'm not exactly come back to life. But I'm walkin' around, hoping to get at Maxton."

"We'll get at him."

"I could put a bullet in him any time. They'd only kill me. Killing's nothing to what they've already done to me."

"No!"

"I guess I'm not ready to die. Funny, ain't it?"

He put an awkward arm about her shoulders. "I want you to live, Rose."

She looked at him, shaking her head. "Why, Doc, you can buy me for a drink and two dollars."

He moved away as from a red hot stove and she laughed. She reached out and touched his hand.

She went on, "Doc, you got to toughen up. You can't stand things the way they are here; you want to clean things up. You got to be real tough."

He said, "We can go away, start over."

"Famous last lines," she jeered.

"It's been done."

"Oh, sure." She began to recite the old ditty born in San Francisco, " 'The miners came in '49, The whores in '51; And when they got together, They produced the native son . . .' That sort of thing, huh? Forget it."

"I won't forget it."

She said, "Has it occurred to you, to change the subject, that Crown was ordered to pick a fight with Ford?"

"Crown works for Carraway."

"Carraway gets along fine with Maxton."

"Ford was a cheater," Sutton said. "He was clumsy when he worked for Maxton, but he's too small, insignificant, for Maxton to worry about."

"You pays your money and you makes your bets." She shrugged and started for the door.

"Sometimes I think we're all crazy. I'd take the stage for California tomorrow if you'd go with me," he said angrily.

She touched his soft whiskers, grinning in sympathy. "Stick around until I need you to check me out. Like you did for Ford."

She slipped out of the door and was gone. Sutton checked his satchel, snapped it shut. He went to the straight chair and sat upon it. He closed his eyes. He shook as though with chills and fever, his long fingers working like small snakes. His teeth were clenched, however, and his feet firmly planted on the wooden floor.

Chapter Four

The saloon where the fight between Paul Crown and Ford, the tinhorn, had started was no more than a cantina. Mexicans huddled around a table in the rear playing monte for coins, as though nothing had happened. Behind the bar was a pockmarked fat man known only as "Mex." The bottle before Dinty Magin and Daniel Logan was half-filled with a good variety of tequila.

Dinty drank and said, "Trouble with Ed Badger, he bought cattle while Mel Carraway was buyin' land. Came the big freeze and Ed hadda go to the bank."

"Peter Mortimer's bank?"

"Formerly Mortimer's bank. Now Simon Maxton's bank."

"He owns the bank, too?"

"Maxton owns about everything. You mind old Mortimer?"

"A dried up skinflint."

"It was sell or fight Maxton. Old Mortimer skedaddled with what he could scrape up and some he stole. Got down to South America, they tell it. Died down there. Young gal got him and he died."

"So now Maxton's the banker and Ed Badger is broke."

"Ed's got his ranch. A few head, enough to live off. But you know how proud he was."

"He taught me to shoot."

"Couldn't of had a better teacher. Ed was some punkins with a Colt. Now he just drinks whiskey."

"And Mel did well."

"Maxton holds a mortgage on Ed's land. Mel figures to buy it up, of course, when he marries Susan. It's that simple." Magin poured another drink. "Mel and Maxton get along. Mel aims to be a big man in New Mexico."

"Maxton allows this?"

"Maxton is a queer fish. Like how much is all this town real estate worth? Where does all the hard cash come from? Cattle comin' up, of course, wetbacks from Mexico, allus did have that. But there's too much hard money around. It don't make sense."

"Is Mel dealing in wetbacks?"

"I couldn't say." Magin was cagey, now. "There's plenty I can't say 'cause I don't know."

"It's a wild town."

"Crazy, is what it is. A tinhorn like Ford gets hisself shot up by Mel's man Paul Crown. Balera puts him in the hoosegow for an hour or two, nothin' else ever happens. Mel puts up bail, the case never comes up."

"Sounds like fun," Logan said. "For Maxton."

"Way I heard it, Ford was aimin' to open a game for hisself, out on the edge of town. Rose Maguire was in on it. But Crown kilt him and Crown's a Carraway man. You go and figure that out."

"I'm just here to buy some cattle and settle down. The way you tell it, I won't be welcome."

"You got enough cash?"

"I think so."

"Just so's you don't borrow from the bank, you'll be all right. Maxton's lookin' for supporters. I told you, he's gettin' political."

"He sounds like somethin', all right. I'll try to keep peaceful around him."

"Gals," said Magin, frowning. "He brings 'em in, gets rid of 'em one way or another. This part of the country ain't ever been much for hifalutin' gals from New York, Chicago, every place. Maxton brings 'em in. He's got a new one from back there, skinny little high-headed one, rides like a native, puts on airs. Maxton's hell on gals."

"And you worry about them?" Logan laughed. "Getting a bit old for that, wouldn't you say?"

"Man never gets too old for that," Magin said. His eyes were bright with liquor. "Wife's been dead five years. No kids to worry about. You mind Mandy?"

"I remember her well." She had been a kindly little woman, quick with cookies and milk.

Magin said, "Never get used to bein' without her." He threw down the tequila. "These gals Maxton brings in, they're no good."

Logan said, "Where would you suggest I buy some stock?"

"Mel Carraway, if he'll sell. Or down Mexico way." Magin waved his hand. "I dunno. They leave me alone, what the hell?"

The old carpenter was showing the effects of the booze, Logan thought. There was no more to be gained by this conversation. The barkeeper was looking worried. "Well, got to stable my horse and change before I eat. Been a long ride. Dandy still operating the barber shop?"

"Dandy's still there. You don't want to drink with me?"

"I've been drinking with you," Logan said gently, putting a coin on the bar. "Better go back and get your corpse ready, hadn't you?"

"Corpuses'll wait. They allus do." Magin poured again. "You run along, Daniel. Don't pay no mind to an old man. Just remember I was your pappy's friend."

"I appreciate it. See you later." He went out of the saloon. Dusk had fallen, suddenly, as always in the valley. He walked down to the hotel and led the black horse to the stable, where an indifferent man named Monterey took his money and turned the animal over to a stable boy. The boy seemed bright and Logan gave him four bits to take special care of the horse.

The barber shop was halfway down the block. Lights were coming on now, such illumination as Logan had never seen in a frontier town. The rawness evaporated, Bailey shone like a jewel amidst the towering ranges. The front of the hotel was bright as a harvest moon as he went up the steps and found his room at the front of the building on the second floor. He drew the shade of the big window and opened his ample bedroll, spreading it on the floor to avoid soiling the newly spread bed.

He had brought only one dark suit with its appurtenances and one change of underwear. He shook out the garments and hung them on hooks set into the wall to let some of the creases shake out. He stripped and poured water and washed himself as best he could, but he needed a shave and a real bath, he knew. He refolded the clean clothing, donned his money belt and Levis and a hickory shirt and took his bundle downstairs and onto the street, heading for Dandy Blewitt's barber shop and public bath. A tall man bumped him on the walk and Logan swung sharply around.

"Sorry, stranger," said the high, nasal voice of Paul Crown. "Didn't look where I was goin'."

"That's all right," Logan said.

The gunslinger squinted in the lights. "You ain't wearin' a gun, mister. You know where you are?"

"I wear a gun sometimes," said Logan.

"Then you better wear one here," said Crown. He laughed, sounding like a mule braying in the night. He walked on toward the livery stable.

Logan continued to the barber shop. The place had been enlarged. There was a room containing a pool table built on to the north side of the old wooden building. Dandy Blewitt, middle-aged, lean, with eyes like poached eggs, string tie, immaculate white shirt and all, grinned at him, showing yellow horse teeth.

"Well, Daniel. Long time since I cut your hair."

"Few years, all right. Can I have a bath first, or would you rather work first?"

"Take your bath. Softens the beard. My razors don't get no sharper, seems like, with the years." The baggy eyes were curous. "You ain't wearin' your Colt."

"People keep complaining about that." Logan was going to the bath house in the rear.

"You home to stay?"

"I'll let you know when I've had my bath." Logan went through the door and locked it behind him. Dandy was honest according to his lights, but there was no guarantee that some wild one might not come in and steal everything a man owned while he was in the bath.

There was a huge, deep wooden tub and above it a tank of heated water. The fire was in the rear, but the room was hot and humid. Logan pulled a chain and water flowed into the big basin. He made it as hot as possible and inserted himself gingerly, cake of soap and wash rag in hand.

It was a good place to think things over. It seemed odd that he had only been in town one afternoon. Already he had seen a man killed and had heard gossip enough to last him for awhile. Maxton, he began to think, was indeed a most dangerous man.

He would look up Mel Carraway tomorrow, he thought. It was safer to begin negotiations for cattle and for rebuilding the old house at once. Maxton was sure to have henchmen at all stations, men armed and ready to work.

Dinty Magin was aging and he was partly scared, it would be best to proceed cautiously with the oldtimer, telling him nothing, believing only part of what Magin said.

Rose Maguire was a sad case. Her dyed blonde hair made her look ancient. She was Logan's age, no more, he remembered. And Dr. Sutton had more than ordinary interest in the beat-up old prostitute. Strange combination, those two, he pondered.

He would have to get off his reports to Barty by mail, put it on the stage himself, he figured. The telegraph would never do, it was odds on Maxton had a record of every wire going out of Bailey.

The whole thing was crazy, he added irritably. Drugs in the west, in the home country, it didn't figure. In New York, Chicago, San Francisco among the Chinese, that was big business. But that it should come from here did not make sense.

As for Barty, he did not own that much land hereabouts. The courthouse did not provide proof among the recorded deeds. Unless there was someone else in on it. Carraway, he wondered? Would the Colonel be playing footsie with Mel and worrying about it and about Maxton's hold on the drug traffic and his influence here?

He had thought there was nothing left of his feeling for home, that it had all gone when his parents died and his own life had come to a low point. Now he began to realize that it was still there. The notion of his home countryside beneath the heel of a Maxton was nauseating.

He closed his eyes to wash his face with soap. When he opened them again he saw the peep hole. It was behind the chair where he had deposited his money belt, ingeniously carved into a dark knot of the wooden wall. He had been careless, he realized.

The damage was done. He pulled the plug and let the water out of the tub and pretended to be oblivious to the fact that he was being watched. He yawned as he donned his clothing, sleepy-eyed, lethargic. He dressed, buckling on the money belt beneath his shirt. While he apparently fumbled with his coat he slipped the derringer into a specially built pocket beneath his waistband. He yawned again, shaking his head as if to dispel sleep.

In the barber shop he glanced around, saw no customers, only a couple of men playing pool in the next room. One was wide and thick-necked and dark. The other was short and quick moving and blond. A third man joined them, a Mexican type with greasy hair and long arms.

Logan climbed into the chair as Dandy Blewitt whisked an apron beneath his chin, deftly secured it, picked up his razor and began stropping.

"How's it been with you, Daniel?"

"Take a little. Leave a little. I see you've expanded."

"Had to. Between the tables and the gals,

I can't stay ahead."

"Still with the tables?"

"I win some. Then I lose it back. Then the gals get to me and I have to win to get somethin' to eat. So, I manage to win."

"Look at the fun you have, breaking even," Logan said.

"Well, I been buckin' the tables a long time. Since you was just a shaver." He smiled fatuously. "Is that a joke? No . . . it should go, 'since I was a shaver' which is a long, long time."

"And you never quit chasin' those gals?"

"Maxton brings in some beauts," Dandy said, approaching with a shaving brush laden with suds. "You run into Simon yet?"

"Not yet."

Dandy fluttered the sharp blade. "Quite a man, quite a man, Simon is. Made this town. It was nothin' until Simon came here, you know that. Nothin' at all."

"You know him well, this Maxton?"

"Well, me playin' the tables the way I do. You get to know the man who owns 'em."

"That's right." Logan closed his eyes. The pool game in the next room was desultory, there seemed no excitement in it.

"Simon treats me good. Even gives me credit when I need it." Dandy sounded defensive.

"Nice for you." The razor scraped but Blewitt had a steady hand. Conversation died for awhile. Dandy finished and wiped away the soap. The pool players had departed.

Blewitt said, "Guess you know your old place is up for taxes. Guess that's why you're back."

"Yes, that's why I'm back. Tomorrow will do."

"I s'pose you got the cash and all."

"You s'pose right.

"Been out that way lately?"

"Why, no," said the barber. "I don't ride out much no more."

"I heard it was used up. People can't be blamed for that, you know," Logan said. "Place stands idle, things happen to it."

"They been grazin' your land," Blewitt said. "Reckon you expected that, too."

"Long as they don't dam off my water," Logan agreed. He saw Dandy wince and guessed that a dam was something he would have to fight against.

Why should he fight a dam, he thought at once? It was only a cover story, stocking the ranch, settling down. He was beginning to believe it himself, which was good for his cover-up but bad for him.

He gave Dandy a dollar and said, "Thanks. See that my dirty duds get to the

Chinaman, will you?"

"That'll be two bits extry. But I pick 'em up for you when they're ready," the barber said.

Logan gave him four bits. "Do that. I'll be seeing you, Dandy."

The barber said, "Daniel."

At the door, Logan paused. "Yes?"

"Lot of tough people in town. You know. People you and me don't savvy. Tough."

Logan glanced toward the empty pool room. "I see what you mean. Thanks again."

Logan was aware of something gnawing at him. It was, he decided, hunger. He went to where a sign said "Cafe — Eats" and entered. It was a small place and a dark-skinned girl was waiting upon three tables, all occupied. In a corner was a tiny round single. Logan went to it and seated himself.

The girl came over, wiping a strand of black Indian hair from her eyes and said in Spanish, "Senor, you cannot sit here, by your leave."

"And why not?" he answered in the same language.

"Because Senor Maxton, he is possible to come and this is his place."

"He comes every night? At this hour?"

"But that is not of the concern. If he should come here, this is where he sits. For the tacos, tortillas, dishes he has not known before."

"Just bring me a tacos and chile relano," he told her. "I will do the worriment about Senor Maxton."

"But I cannot," she cried. She was close to tears. "It will go badly with my mama, with me, with Pedro."

"Is it Pedro who works in the hotel?"

"The same."

Logan said, "Is there space in the kitchen, perhaps?"

"But the senor would not eat in the kitchen!"

He got up, bowed, and said to her, "If you will lead the way, senorita?"

They went through a door behind a burlap curtain. The kitchen was larger than the dining space. An ancient lady was cooking, wiping sweat from her brow with a bandanna. The girl spouted at her, the woman turned.

"Ah, it is you, Senor Daniel," she said. "Welcome home."

"Perdita? Is that you, Perdita?"

"What is left of me," she said. There was a tooth missing in the front of her smile. Ten years ago she had been a nice looking young wife and mother. Her husband, Pete Rugelo, had worked on the ranches in roundup time, trying to put together a small spread of his own the rest of the year, farming, trucking.

"And my amigo, Pete?"

"Dead and gone these eight years," she said. "I am here, in this place, since then. My daughter, Consuelo, this is Senor Daniel Logan."

The girl said, "But mama. Senor Maxton, he comes through here to eat, perhaps."

"No problem," Daniel Logan told her. "Maxton never saw me before."

"But that is the problem," said the girl. "Senor Maxton, he does not like strangers." Then she cried, "Aieee! Mama!"

Logan had already noted the side door, leading from an alley between the restaurant and Maxton's place. Now the three men came in, with guns in their hands, the blond, the dark man and the Mexican.

The derringer had only two shots and there was the problem of the women. Still, these three might kill anyone who might witness against them. He shot the leader, the dark man, between the eyes. He shot the second in line, the blond, hitting the bridge of his nose. He lunged at the Mexican, then leaped aside, across the room, barely in time to avoid a cascade of boiling water.

Mama Rugelo had thrown a pan with

utmost accuracy. The Mexican howled as he went backwards. Another shot sounded and the remaining thief fell dead on the kitchen floor. A man walked in holding a nickel-plated .38 revolver in his hand. He was a very large man in black broadcloth, with a hard eastern hat, a white stock and a flowered vest.

"Senor Maxton!" murmured Consuelo.

Mama Rugelo said quickly, "This is a friend, Senor. This is an old friend, Senor Logan."

Maxton's face was round and full. His cheeks were pink and his eyes a deep, piercing brown. He was heavyset and flatfooted, a pillar of strength and health. He said, "Logan? You're the rancher come home, ain't you?"

Logan was fitting lead into his derringer. "That's right. Simon Maxton, isn't it?"

"Looks like I got hungry just in the nick of . . ." said Maxton, shoving the revolver into his pocket without blowing out the smoke nor reloading. He leaned out the door and yelled, "Buffalo! You Buffalo! Get Sunny and come over here with your broom and shovel. Call Magin, too. There's work to do. Hustle your scut, now."

Mama Perdita was already putting on a fesh pan of water. Blood was running on the boards and the girl was against the far wall, pale as her apron. Maxton kicked each of the prone men to make certain there was no life in them.

"Shot him in the back. That sounds bad," he said to nobody in particular. "Is it all right to shoot a thief in the back?"

Logan said, "He was pretty well scalded at the time. But he did have a gun in his hand."

Maxton bent to peer, said, "Say, he still has got it in his mitt. You're all witnesses. Right?"

"You are right, Senor," said Perdita smoothly. "You have save our life."

"Well, now." Maxton beamed at Logan. "You eat yet?"

"Just about to."

"Consuelo, put another chair at my table," Maxton ordered. "You can eat with me, Logan." He started for the dining room.

Logan said, "Thanks. But I'll stay and see that the kitchen's cleaned."

"But I asked you to eat with me." Maxton was puzzled. "It's somethin' I never do."

"I wouldn't have you inconvenienced for worlds," Logan told him. "Just go ahead. I'll join you for a drink, perhaps."

Maxton scowled. He looked older, different, ugly when he frowned. "You don't want to eat with me?"

"I just killed two men," said Logan. "It takes a few minutes for my stomach to settle."

Maxton's face cleared, he grinned. "Squeamish, huh? Well, like you say. See you in a little while." He waved at Consuelo. "The usual, my dear. I ain't squeamish, but I am damn hungry."

The girl's hands were shaking worse than ever. Perdita lifted one shoulder, looked at Logan, then turned to the stove. It was not a time for conversation.

Logan led the girl to the sink, poured water, took out a small vial, gave her a pill. "Something new. The doctors call it 'aspirin' and it calms the nerves." He swallowed one of the white tablets himself to prove they were not poisonous. The girl followed suit and was impressed, her eyes big and round, gulping.

Perdita said, "Those three. Better off dead."

"You know them?"

"They are new. They came from the south, from Old Mexico. Two, three days. They lose all at the tables. So they must steal."

A very small and scruffy Indian put his head in the door, then stepped aside as the two Teutonic, stolid, muscle men who worked for Magin came in and began hauling out the dead men without offering a word. The Indian had the broom and dustpan of the saloon swamper. Perdita handed him a mop, indicated a pail and the Indian went to work cleansing the floor. Logan accepted a cup of strong coffee. Business as usual, that was the motto of Bailey, he thought.

He was not really "squeamish" nor was his nerve easily affected. He had expected an attack by the three men. He had killed before, more than once, more than a dozen times in the pursuit of his line of work. He felt no compunction about ridding the world of three thieves who were unquestionably murderers.

Consuelo said, "But I do feel better. Gracias, Senor Logan. The pill, it works well."

Aspirin, he thought, something they had discovered back East. Not a panacea, but good for headaches and other minor pains. He needed a large dose, not because of the dead men, but because Simon Maxton had Bailey in his claws and it was going to be a Herculean task to turn the town loose.

There were bottles of wine racked against the wall in a crib. He selected one, gave a gold coin to Perdita, waved away her move to give him change.

"I can eat, now," he told her. "The great caballero awaits."

She put her finger to her lips, whispered in Spanish, "You will be careful?"

"Very careful." Carrying the wine, he went into the restaurant. Maxton was seated against the wall at the small table. There was another chair and Logan sat down, uncorking the wine with a deft gesture.

"Consuelo will be here at once," he told the big man. "She was a bit unsettled, you understand."

Chawing on brittle bits of tacos, Maxton grunted. "Didn't hear me yell, eh? Got to think of other people. Comes hard, sometimes. I'm a man used to service."

"So I understand." Logan poured wine into water glasses already upon the table.

"You know about me, eh?" Maxton's voice was harsh and flat with a New York intonation, his speech was half literate, half guttersnipe.

"Your name's pretty prominent around town."

"And Dinty Magin's got a big mouth."

"Then you've heard about me?"

"I got my sources. Meant to look you up soon. You might need a loan from the bank if you're settlin' down on the Rockin' Chair."

81

"You have heard," Logan said. "Thanks, I won't need a loan. Got lucky down in Texas."

"Lucky? You a gambler?" Maxton's brow was low, his hair grew down upon it in coarse furze. "You'll be playin' my tables, then."

"No," said Logan. "I deal. Or I play head and head poker. I'm not in need of a dealing job. I'll be too busy to stay up all night."

"That's right smart," said Maxton. "You're the kind of man we need. Like Mel Carraway. Business, all business."

"Yes, all business."

"You don't talk like no westerner," Maxton remarked. "You been east?"

"Several times," said Logan.

"N' Yawk?" There was a sudden wariness in the man.

"Certainly, New York. Would anyone go east without seeing New York?"

Maxton asked, "Spend much time there?"

"Enough to see the elephant. It's a lovely, pink, friendly elephant."

"Ha! That's the way you seen it."

"I was there to have fun," Logan told him.

"You gamble any there?"

"No," lied Logan. "We stayed pretty much uptown."

"You said 'we.' You married?"

"No." Maxton would learn about Susan soon enough, he knew. "Never had the time, since I left here."

"There'll be a weddin' here next week. Mel Carraway. I guess you know about that."

"I heard. I didn't know it was to take place so soon."

"Good man, Carraway. Never did cotton to whores. Business, all business. Well, it's been very nice meetin' you. Dinner's paid for. See you tomorrow?"

"Could be. Good evenin'," said Logan.

He watched the man walk out of the restaurant through the front door, splay-footed but with a certain ponderous dignity. Just the type, Logan thought, to come into the west, corrupt the countryside and run for Senator . . . and win. It had been done time and again in the new land. People forgot too easily, or didn't care. The Maxtons took their money, spent a few dollars back on them, then got elected. It was a sickening thought.

Then he remembered that he had never in his life roosted long enough to vote. He was here for Colonel Barty, not to clean up the town of Bailey. He had been paid in advance and he had an obligation to get ahead with his mission.

He went into the kitchen again, moved close to Mama Rugelo and spoke in Spanish, quietly.

"Those three. From the south, you say?"

"Of a certainty. Coming to carry a message to Senor Maxton," she replied.

"To Maxton? From whom did they bring a message?"

"That I do not know. There are often messengers from the south. This is known to many. From Mexico, from Texas. This is important to Senor Maxton."

"Important in what way?"

"Money," she answered. "Three things are vastly important to Senor Maxton. Money. Women. Politics."

"And food."

"Si, food. Four things." She smiled, showing the gap in her teeth. "He is a big man in this place. I feed him. He pays."

"But you do not care for him very much."

"Is it necessary I should care for my customers?"

"No, certainly not. But I may ask questions from time to time. You will be well paid for answering them. Does that suit you?"

"If you are discreet. I cannot afford trouble, even for an old friend. I have Pedro and Consuelo, I must see to their welfare."

He gave her another goldpiece. "Discretion is the key to the entire matter. I will see you another time. Hasta luego."

CHAPTER FIVE

The stage came in from Silver City about noon. From it descended a woman in a tweed suit, wearing stout boots and smoking a cigar. She was greeted with warmth by the Wells Fargo agent, the hotel manager and bystanders as, "Annie Morgan, how be you?" "How's the lady drummer?"

She distributed samples of El Ropo, the cheapest twist of tobacco in her line and moved to the register, which she examined with great care. She had merry blue eyes and a firm chin surprisingly dotted with a dimple. She signed for a room with a flourish, took her sample case from Pedro, gave him a two bit piece and walked across to Maxton's Palace.

A few men were drinking their lunch. Behind the bar loomed Sunny Tate, a barrel of a man with a broad grin which seemed painted onto his rocklike features.

"Sunny, how are you?" sang out Annie Morgan. "Simon in his office?"

"Sure enough, Miss Annie. Go right on

up." Sunny waved a hand like a roast of beef.

She climbed a flight of stairs which wound around into a balcony off which there were several rooms behind closed doors. At the end of the balcony she paused and rapped with plump knuckles, using a certain tattoo. The door was opened by Buffalo, the Indian swamper, who was smoking a perfecto. She entered, setting down her case near the door, and dropped into an empty chair at a round mahogany table.

Simon Maxton sat opposite her. Buffalo sat at her side, a silent, sharp-eyed little Apache, no hint of the swamper about his demeanor. Tanner was next to Buffalo, a lean man in dandified range clothing, wearing a revolver tied low on his thigh and a Bowie knife in fringed leggings. On the other side of Maxton was Mose Johnson, squat, flat headed, scarred from a hundred fights in the prize ring, black as the ace of spades, coatless to display a revolver encased in a shoulder holster.

Annie Morgan said, "Hail, hail, the gang's all here. And how are my merry friends?"

"Worried," said Maxton. "What news do you bring, Annie?"

"The Colonel is worried, too." She slumped in the chair, surprisingly delicate fingers tapping the tabletop. "The take has fallen off, hasn't it, gents?"

"It has indeed," said Maxton. The others kept their eyes on Annie, unsmiling. "Where's the stuff?"

She motioned to the sample case. "I brought in what we could get hold of. Not near enough. It's been cut, too. Came in by New Orleans. What's the matter with our friends below the border?"

"We thought you'd know about him."

She shook her head. "Simon, Simon! El Puma is your man. You brought him in. Greatest thing since Christmas trees, you said. More stuff than a thousand cokies could dream of every month. Safe as a dollar bill. Just give you protection from the District Office, you said. Make us all rich in a year."

"It was working when he started reneging. He wants all the money. Sure, I had words with him. But he promised to come through this month. We just got word he was down around Mexico City. Just that, nothing else. Why? Why is he acting up?"

"That's our question." She didn't change her position, but her voice grew cold and harsh. "You're doing all right here, all of you. The Colonel's not doing so well for the risk he's taking. You haven't come up with title to the mining properties, the ranches, the grazing."

"We were going to give him Rocking Chair," Maxton said. "Logan came in and paid off the tax this morning."

"Logan? Who's Logan?"

"He owned the place, inherited it. We couldn't prevent him from pickin' up the taxes, could we?"

Annie Morgan said, "All we know is that you make excuses and we don't get a decent cut. How much is it this time?"

There was a silence. She mused aloud, "I told the Colonel it would be like this. Too much going for you, Simon. He should have had someone up here watching for the moment. He trusted you. He's going to be terribly disappointed."

Maxton said, "He got plenty out of us."

"He set you up. He brought you out here. Haven't you got any gratitude?"

"He's got plenty going for him in Texas and Arizona. I'm not gonna cry any tears for the Colonel."

"But he'll take it hard," she pointed out. "Ambrose won't like it, either. And I'm not so sure El Puma will go along with you."

"We take chances," Maxton said. "Been takin' chances all my life. I'm figurin' to get into politics, Annie. Tell the Colonel that."

"You mean you're going to let me out of town alive?" She was genuinely surprised.

Maxton nodded to Mose Johnson, who shoved back his chair and went to the sample case and brought it back, placing it on the table.

"Just so long as you don't make a fuss."

"That's stealing," she said, shaking her head. "Stealing from the Colonel. There's a few thousand in drugs in that bag."

"We need a slush fund, for the politickin'," Maxton told her seriously. "You got to buy votes, you know that."

"Simon, you amaze me. You really do." She fumbled with her purse, took out a fresh cigar, lit it. She blew smoke across the table. "If I don't shut up, you'll have me killed. If I go home empty-handed, the Colonel will probably kill me. Hell of a thing to happen to a woman, now, isn't it?"

"You can take care of yourself."

She said, "Not here. Not in Bailey. And not in El Paso with old faithful Ambrose around and about."

"You want a stake, Annie? You want to get out of the country, maybe?"

"I got too much invested," she complained. "Just peddling cigars, I make a living. Where else can I do that?"

"Well, what you got on your mind?"

"I'll have to think. I'll just stick around awhile, until something comes to me. Is that okay?"

"You want to join up, don't you, Annie? You figure you'll be safer here as long as the Colonel ain't wise. You're a popular dame, You could get me some votes."

Annie said, "Give me time, will you?"

Maxton looked around the table. The others had not uttered a sound. Now they all gave the briefest of nods.

Maxton said, "We'll be watchin', you know. We watch pretty good in Bailey. You make your rounds. You play it slow and easy. You check with us. Then you tell us your notions. You got a brain, Annie, we know that. We'd be fools if we didn't use your brain, if you'll play straight with us. But you got to remember those mountains out there got deep holes, ravines, whatever. A body could lay out there a long time, 'specially if nobody's lookin' for it very hard."

Annie said, "What can I do? I'll play it your way. Maybe I can think up something. Just a little something to save old Annie's hide."

She got up, twirling the cigar. Even now she was smiling. "I suspected this, like I told you. The way you've been going here, why should you cut in anyone? But I'll give you

90

a piece of advice." She indicated the sample case. "Send the Colonel some kind of a cut. He can be a bad, bad actor when his dander's up. Really bad."

"Sure, Annie, girl, we know," said Maxton. "But you never seen us when we're actin' bad."

She flipped open the case, took out display boxes of the tobacco line, pried a false bottom loose and dumped tightly wrapped packages from it. "I need the samples," she explained. "Happy days, gents."

She closed the bag and waved at them and left the room. Tanner touched one of the packages and lifted a brow. Mose Johnson opened it, spilled white crystals.

"She wouldn't dare cross us now," Maxton said. "She don't know we got to put her away. She's smart enough to know she can't go back to El Paso. Let her stick around awhile, what harm?"

"She knows too much," said Tanner.

"Who's she going to tell?"

"The Colonel? By mail?"

"That's one of the chances we take," Maxton decided. "I wouldn't mind if he did send Ambrose. We can take care of Ambrose, can't we?"

They agreed. Buffalo spoke suddenly, "I watch plenty. I watch mails, too. I steal letter she write."

"Good," said Maxton. "That's the way to do it. Now, let's package this stuff for mailin' east."

They went to a closet and took out metal containers and began filling them, sealing them with hot wax.

Logan walked down toward the livery stable, replete with eggs, refried beans and bacon. The deed to Rocking Chair was filed at the courthouse — a one-room building at the end of Main Street — and he intended to ride out and spend the afternoon reconnoitering his property. A carriage rolled into the yard.

"Daniel," said a clear voice well remembered. "Daniel, what in the world?"

He trailed the reins and walked toward her. He saw Mel Carraway, then holding the reins, his broad face alert, not quite certain at the moment, staring with wide-spaced pale eyes.

"Susan, how are you . . . Mel, congratulations."

She came down and held his elbows, looking up at him. She was all woman, deep-bosomed, blonde hair caught up beneath a fetching bonnet, deep blue eyes compelling, the mouth curved and strong. He was shocked by the coursing of his blood at her touch, he had not expected that.

"Daniel David Logan. You're home!"

"Just got in yesterday." He felt foolish, mouthing commonplace words, remembering how it had been, how she had lain all soft and compliant in his arms. "Paid the tax, thought I'd go out and look around."

Mel Carraway handed the reins to the boy and came down, a big fellow, just Daniel Logan's age, thick-chested, heavy of arm and leg, dressed in cords, looking every inch the prominent rancher and citizen, humorless always.

"Glad to have you back, Dan. It's been a long time. Where in the world have you been all these years?"

"Oh, up and down and here and there. Lots of places."

"You and Luke Short?" Mel asked. "We heard you were good friends."

"Luke's a good man," said Logan. "We did a few things together. He's a sharp gambler."

"You've been a gambler?" The blue eyes clouded. "I am surprised, Daniel."

"It's a way of life," he said humbly. "Luke's on the square, you know. We mostly dealt or bucked the big wigs with bankrolls."

"Nothin' wrong with it," Mel said in his

blunt fashion. "Too chancy for me, but nothin' agin it. Me, I stick to land. Had a notion to buy in your place if you wasn't going to pay the taxes."

"Why not? It's good land, good water."

"I been grazin' your pastures," said Carraway. "I'll want to talk to you about the water, you know, them things."

"No problem," disclaimed Logan. "Glad you used the land, Mel. No sense lettin' it lay fallow."

Susan said, "Mel's doing very well. We're building a new house." There was something mechanical in her announcement, and Logan looked curiously at her. In that instant he knew that the old current was there, ready to be turned on as in the days gone by. It was, surprisingly, a disturbing and depressing thought.

"Well, don't let me keep you," he said. "Maybe we can get together for supper?"

"We'll be in town all day," Mel said in his positive manner. "If you get back in, look for us."

"Yes, Daniel. I want to hear everything, all about you, what you plan to do at Rocking Chair. We will be neighbors, after all."

He watched them walk away, noting that Mel tucked Susan's arm beneath his elbow in proprietary fashion. She was tall, but

Carraway was well over six feet, an impressive figure of a man.

Logan mounted and rode north on the road. He held the black horse to a walk, climbing Mob Hill, coming down to where the ranches stretched out side by side, Carraway's and his own and Ed Badger's. Once he had walked every foot of this world, hunted and fished and just tramped with other boys or by himself. He had known it intimately, as only a boy can know a place, the rocks and dirt and grama grass and brush and running water was all his in that time.

He greeted each rise in the terrain, each sloping plain, each turn of the trail with pleasure. He deliberately rode around Mob Hill and to the west, so that he would come first to the Cross B. Ed Badger came clear to his memory, a lean, sturdy man, the true westerner, the perfect gentleman, the horseman, the fast gun, the unerring rifle shot, purveyor of the lore of cougar hunting, trout fishing, the soul of honor. Logan's father had loved this man, had sought his advice upon everything, had been as close as a brother to him.

Daniel David Logan came to the last of the rolling hills and reined in, savoring the panorama. The land lay fair, the grass was lush, stretching east and south across a fertile plain. This was home.

But he could not think of home, he told himself. He was not yet a man for home-coming. He had a job to do, which reduced to its essentials was little more than assas-sination. Colonel Barty and the government in Washington wanted information regard-ing drug traffic and murder. And Barty wanted Maxton dead.

It had not been explicit, of course. Barty was a very careful man. However it was there, it went along with the extra cash from Barty's pocket. Maxton had to be cut down, his ring destroyed, so that the Colonel could command whatever it was he wanted in Bailey County. There could be no surcease for Daniel David Logan until he had ac-complished the task for which he had sold his gun.

He rode down the hill, turning off at a road marked by two old posts. The sign with the Cross B brand on it had been drilled by bullet holes. He swore under his breath at whoever had pumped lead into it and turned up the lane leading to the house beyond the hillock, nestled on the lee side, a rambling, one-storied adobe with a tile roof, tile imported from Mexico.

When it came within view he again reined

in. His heart ached at sight of the sagging porch, the canted chimney, the blistering paint. The place seemed to have shrunk, the corral was too close to the barn, the foothills seemed to have closed in, threatening.

Pathetically, against this disrepair the windows were clean and sparkling with curtains fresh and bright. There was the scratched earth of a tiny garden in the yard, a plot of flowering cacti next to flat stones which led to the porch.

Logan went up the steps. "Hello, Ed."

Badger sat down hard, almost lost his balance, then seemed to regain partial sobriety. His eyes were rheumy, the veins in his prominent nose enlarged, the cheeks mottled. He was unkempt, but he managed to stiffen his neck and stare hard at Logan.

He said, "Susan ain't here," shaking his head as if to dispel shadows.

"I saw her in town," Logan told him. "With Mel."

"Ain't you goin' to sit down?"

There was no other chair. Logan perched on the top step. "How are you, Ed?"

"I'm fine. Fine. Country's goin' to hell. But I just watch it go and . . . I'm fine."

Logan said, "That's good. I heard about Susan and Mel."

"That why you come back?" There was a

small, deep light in the sad hound's eyes for a moment.

"No. Thought I'd buy some stock and settle down. On the old place."

The light vanished. "Settle down in this gofforsaken country? Don't be loco."

"It looks about the same to me. Except Bailey, of course. Bailey is something else again."

"Bailey's a sinkhole. Mel, now, he ain't the same. You'll note that. He's big, Mel is. Biggest in the county." Badger winked. "In the county, mind you. Not in the city. Not there. Thinks he's big there. Not big there."

"I gathered that. Man name of Maxton is big in town."

"Biggest. Maxton." The oddly young hand fumbled for the jug. "Have a toddy, Daniel? No? Too early for you, I'spect."

"You running much stock, Ed?"

"Stock? Critters, you mean? Ha! You heard of the big freeze, Daniel? You heard of that?"

"Sure. It was four years ago."

"Yep. Four years. You know how old I was, then? You know that?"

"Wouldn't have the slightest notion."

Badger lifted the cup and drank. He wiped his lips and said, "Forty-eight, that's how old. Now I'm fifty-two. I'm old, Daniel. I'm finished. Tuckered out."

"That's pretty damn silly."

"Is it? Ask Mel."

"What the hell would he know about it?"

"Ask Susan, then. Old man, they say, you're through. We'll take over the place, add it to Lazy Dog. Make it pay. Just let the bank foreclose. Title will be attended to, goes to Mel and Susan. Set on the porch and enjoy yourself, they say. You done your part." He laughed sourly. "You know what I done, don't you, Daniel?"

"No. I can't even begin to figure this."

"I bought cattle. They froze to death. Mel, he bought land. Land thawed out, cattle didn't. I told Maxton off, plenty, one fine day. Mel, he partnered with Maxton. Now you see why this country's gone to hell?"

"I begin to get a notion."

"Success," said Ed Badger, his voice growing stronger. "Mel, he bought out all the little people. The squatters come in and him and Maxton mortgaged 'em. Got 'em without firin' a shot, they can't make a move without askin' if it's okay with Maxton and Mel. Three ranches left in the valley, mine, yours and Mel's. Lotsa land around, all bought up by Maxton or Mel. Now what? They got me. I'm mortgaged, too."

"When do they foreclose on you?" asked Logan.

"What difference?"

Logan waited a moment, then asked, "You telling me that you quit, Ed?"

"Ha!" It was an old habit, using this expletive in varying tones to mean various things. Badger took another swig from the tin cup and was silent.

"I mind the day nobody cowed Ed Badger."

"The day of the gun is past. This here's the day of lawin' on your neighbor. The day of lendin' money and grabbin' property in exchange. Quit? Supposin' your flesh and blood turned agin you? Supposin' your future son-in-law sets the pace? What you goin' to do, Daniel Logan? Shoot 'em?"

"I withdraw the suggestion," said Logan. "Tell me, Ed, how much stock does Mel run on Lazy Dog?"

"Two, three hundred head. Sometimes. Other times he runs a thousand."

"How's that again?"

"They move in, they move out. He don't raise 'em, he deals in 'em."

"Wetbacks?"

"You want to ask him about that?"

"The day might come," said Logan. "You think he might sell me some cows?"

100

"Strictly speakin', that's about what he could sell you right now. That's what he's got. Milch cows. And a few head of prime stock he keeps around for show. Kinda funny thing, there ain't no cattle in the valley. Just money. Mortgages and money in Bailey. You study on that, Daniel. Study good on it."

Logan hesitated, unwilling to divulge his thoughts on the subject to the older man. "That's interesting. Awhile ago you said the day of the gun was over. But in Bailey I saw a cowboy named Crown shoot down a tinhorn gambler named Ford and go scot free in a couple of hours."

"Did, eh?" Badger drank again. He was rapidly losing concentration, now. "Crown, eh? That's Mel's man. Almost fast, Crown is. Tough, too. He ain't nervish, you know?"

"Why does Mel need him?"

Badger's eyes grew owlish. "Ha! You know Mel. He's plumb slow. Fist fighter, Mel is. Guns? No good."

"So Mel hires his gun. Is it because he doesn't trust his business partner, maybe?"

"Maxton," said Badger. "Maxton has got a gun and a knife workin' for him. And lots of other people. Paul Crown ain't a patch on the Maxton people. You wanta know about Crown? Ask Mel. When you ask him about wetbacks, ask him about Crown."

"Okay," said Logan. "One more question, Ed. Do you known Miguel de Santa Ferra?"

"Son," said Badger, his voice now slurred, "I may be old and I may be finished, but I don't forget. El Puma. The raider. The eddicated fool."

"Fool?"

"Keep runnin' the border, son, and you're askin' for the troops. Ask for the troops and they'll gitcha."

"You mean El Puma has been up this far?"

"Ha!"

"I see." Logan arose. "I'll be moseyin' along, Ed. And I'll be studying on . . . everything."

Logan went to the barn and mounted the black horse. The man on the porch was asleep again. The shadow of the house fell longer than was proper, Logan thought, and the shadow of the barn was enormous. The sun shone bright, but the aura of the Cross B was darker than night. He rode swiftly toward the trail which led to Rocking Chair, not noticing the small game which fled before the hoofs of the horse nor the cottonwoods which loomed alongside the one stream of the valley, the stream which was on his own land.

Miles before he reached the stone house,

unique in that country, he saw the broken chimney. His father had dragged that stone from rimrock and built the house upon a knoll. He came closer and saw that no glass remained in the windows, which was no surprise. The stone stood firm, the yard was overgrown and there was debris of human leaving around, but he had known riders would use the place and expected no more. He tied up to a sapling at water's edge and walked across the yard, slow and thoughtful. He stood for a long moment before entering past the sagging door half off its hinges.

The sight of the interior shocked him out of his lethargy. The floors were stained and hacked. There were bullet holes in the plaster his father had laid over the rough stone interior. The ceilings were ruined, plaster hanging in sheets. The furniture had long been stored, but the wreck of what had been his mother's pride and joy was devasting.

He went into the kitchen. The rusted stove tumbled in upon itself. The pump had been dismantled, the sink hung crooked against the wall. The sills were hacked, the door had vanished.

This was pure vandalism. Someone had deliberately wrecked the home. The wonder was that it had not been gutted by fire. He looked out back toward the small bunk-house of frame. It was apparently intact.

There was a message here somewhere, he thought, his mind switching back to its accustomed groove. He had been acting the homecoming citizen, now he must begin to think in terms to which he had long been inured.

He went out the rear and toward the bunkhouse. It had probably been used from time to time by work hands who were kept from home on winter nights. There was no harm in this. They had taken care not to harm it, there were no broken windows, there was order, with bunks standing against the walls, blankets folded atop them. He stood in the center of the floor.

A voice commanded, "Hold it right there, mister."

He raised his hands part way and without turning said, "It's me. Logan. I own this place."

A girl's husky voice said, "I might have known. You're sudden, Dan."

He asked, unbelieving, "Dora Bell?"

"One and the same," she acknowledged. "Surprised to see me? Hell, I found out you had property here and when New York got hot, I just came along."

He said, "You did what?"

"Well, Maxton hired me. I knew him, of course. It's quite a story, ain't it?"

She had a dancer's walk, going to where she had left her horse alongside the bunkhouse. He watched her mount with ease and grace and wave to him as she rode out. Then he mounted and rode after the girl from New York who had once helped him and Luke Short escape from a wolf den in which they had caused trouble and some bloodshed. It was, he thought, probably the best lead he had since coming to town. Dora Bell was of the underworld, she had seen the elephant and knew all the ropes.

CHAPTER SIX

The last quarter mile, after leaving the clear running blue stream, was across shale. Logan caught up to her and led the way, pleased with the sure-footed black. The rented hack upon which the small girl perched skidded and floundered a bit, but they made it to the cave. They dismounted and led the animals into the high-ceilinged hole in what appeared to be solid rock.

"Golly," said Dora Bell, "it's like one of them books."

There were flat rocks, dragged into position years ago by young hands, Logan well knew. They sat upon them and looked down at the rivulet below and the mountains in the distance, always the mountains of New Mexico. They could see a promontory upon which a nun seemed to kneel, and beyond it a peak shaped like the head of an Indian warrior. The clouds played, fleecy and fat, around the tallest spires.

"What books?" asked Logan. He did not know whether to be amused or annoyed with this waif from the gutters of America's biggest city. He knew he must use her, but in the meantime it was necessary to gain her confidence.

"You know. Ned Buntline. Buffalo Bill. Wild Bill. Injuns."

"Indians, we call them. Usually by their right names, Apaches or Arapahoe or Comanche or Sioux. And Buntline is a fool and a liar and some other things. Those books are the worst fictions ever perpetrated on the public."

She looked at him, unsmiling. "You were in Bailey last night. I seen you. From upstairs, where I was watchin'. You saw Paul and Ford fight. And you tell me them books is lies?"

He collapsed against the wall. "All right, Dora, all right. We do have some goin's on.

Billy the Kid really lived in Silver City — although he did not knife a man in defense of his mother's honor. Pat Garrett shot him over at Maxwell's ranch. Okay. Have it your way."

She said, "And I seen you and Luke down a crooked dealer in New York."

"He pulled a knife on Luke."

"But you shot him."

"I shot him." The battle was lost. "So you came out here hoping to find some more fun?"

"Excitement," she said primly. She could alter her aspect like a chameleon on a piece of Scotch plaid. "And besides, I got in Dutch."

"On account of helping us?"

"That started it. They got suspicious. I was holdin' out on them, you see."

"I see. Saving your money to come west."

"That's right. So, when they caught me, I was ready. I was on that choo choo whilst they were lookin' all over Five Points." She laughed like a gay youngster. "Maxton, he'd got into trouble with Tammany Hall, and they were after him, so he left. A few of us knew where he went and then I wrote some letters from Chi. It's easy to get the names of land owners if you know how. Then I thought, well, you would either turn up or you wouldn't and why not?"

"What did you expect from me?"

Her eyes were round and large and very direct. "Why, Logan, you couldn't run out on me after I saved you and little Luke back there, now, could you?"

"But what could I do for you?" He recovered quickly and added, "I mean, what *can* I do for you?"

"What I want is a gamblin' house, a swell one, see? With mirrors on the walls and carpet on the floor. Roulette, faro, chuck-a-luck, poker tables, dice, everything fancy. And straight."

"Luke Short's your man for that, down in Fort Worth," he told her. "He went there when he left Tombstone. That's the kind of place he's opening there."

She grinned at him. "Luke would put me to work. Right? Nice little fella, Luke. But would he want competition? No. What I want, I want a start in the right place. I got the loot, Logan. I got plenty. All I need is a muscle."

"I see. I'm to be the muscle."

"You're to be my partner. You pick the spot, give me protection and you're in for halfies." She beamed upon him. "You like it?"

He stared at her. "Why, Dora, it's the best

proposition I've had this week!"

"Good. When do we start?"

He said, "But I own a ranch down there. I'm settling down, buying cattle, rebuilding the house."

"Well think hard. Maxton ain't goin' to like it."

"So?"

"Oh, you ain't afraid, I know that. But Maxton, he's already settled in. He's gettin' bigger than anybody knows."

"On the drug trade." He shot it at her flatly.

"Oh." She sighed and crossed her knees. "You know."

"It's my home town," he said, covering himself as best he could. She was amazingly quick and clever, he realized. "I, too, ask questions."

"Dinty Magin." She nodded. "Seen you talkin' to him up and down the street. That was kinda dumb. Maxton's people watch everywhere. Magin's scared of his life."

"Yes, I thought so. Look, if you're not involved in that . . . But you're not."

"I deal," she said. "Maxton's after me all the time, but he knows I just deal. And drink with the fancy dudes who might need booze before they play."

"How does Maxton bring it in?"

"I don't want to know," she told him. She had lost the brightness and anticipation she had brought to the interview. "You're some kind of cop, huh?"

"No," he said. "Or — maybe yes. They pay me to look into things. I couldn't arrest you if I caught you robbing the bank."

"Secret stuff?"

"That's it. Maxton's double crossing somebody and I'm paid to learn what's going on. It's that simple."

She started to lead the horse from the cave. She paused and said, "Fort Worth, was it? Where Luke is, I mean?"

"That's right. Nice town, railroads crisscrossing through it, everything modern, like New York. Artificial ice, girl's school, Benedictine Academy, everything."

"Some wild west," she said disconsolately. "Okay, Logan. I'll be around awhile, until I can make a clean getaway from Maxton. He's hot after me, but he's too busy to really go to work on me right now. Maybe you can gimme a hand on blowin' the burg, huh?"

"Any time," he assured her. "And I promise not to speak to you in Bailey. You'd better go ahead, alone. Only two people know about this cave. They're in town."

"Susan Badger and Carraway," she said.

"You played here when you was kids."

"Now, how did you know that?"

"Easy," she said. "You keep lookin' around, mooncalfy. The rocks, they were put here, long time ago. Mention her name and you get all goosey."

"Mooncalfy? Goosey?"

"Carraway, he was a kid then, too. So he was part of it. Wantin' her but knowin' you had the inside track."

"Magin told you!"

She said, "Logan, I don't know about you. Sometimes I think you're like, well, a hero fella. Then you act like some hecker from Peanutsville." She made her graceful mount, held the reins loose, looking down at him. "I had notions about you, Logan. I really did. But now . . . I'm too young to be a widow again. So long, sucker."

She rode across the shale toward the stream down in the valley. He leaned against the wall of the cave, watching her. He felt as though someone had stuck a needle into him and extracted a lot of juice. He was too taken aback to even be angry.

She was the strangest female he had ever encountered. Her intuition was remarkable, he thought, and her brain like that of a man . . . an intelligent man. She had the courage and initiative of a man, too. Yet she was certainly not masculine. In fact, she was cute as a bug's ear.

He should have questioned her with more vigor, perhaps. But he had noted the light dim within her and sensed that she was inwardly disturbed, discouraged. Her fear of Maxton and his people was very real. The best thing she could do would be to get on that stage and start eastward for Fort Worth. Luke was always amiable to the ladies. She and the little dude gambler would make a great pair.

He left the cave and rode over a hill, still thinking about the odd little girl from New York. The plain lay before him, grama grass bright where a small ditch from the main stream had been dug across the pasture land in the days when the Carraways and the Logans had been close friends. He saw a herd, a few hundred short-horned, squat head, a seed herd, he thought, developed over the years by a careful intelligence. Prime stock, no question about it, he added. Mel Carraway was dealing in futures. He rode down toward the meadow and back to town.

CHAPTER SEVEN

Colonel Barty sat behind his desk as usual. Ambrose leaned against the wall in his favorite spot. There was a tap on the door and the older brother motioned with his head. Ambrose went to what appeared to be a wall cabinet, moved it so that it swung to reveal a closet-like hole, stepped inside, swung the cabinet back into place.

Barty got up and went to the alley door and opened it. Miguel de Santa Ferra, alias El Puma, swaggered into the office, clad in somber black town garments, smoking a cigarillo.

"Good evenin', Senor," Barty said, unsmiling. "Take a chair."

The Mexican dandy sat, one hip eased to show the bulge of a revolver quick to his hand. "How are you, Colonel?"

"I been better, Senor. Matter of Simon Maxton. You and him have got pretty thick, haven't you?"

"Thick? Why, not exactly. Business, y' know. Must be gracious to a business fella."

"Me, I'm a business fella, too."

"True. Very true. But devious. Can't always know what you're about now, can we?"

Barty said, "I been financin' you and

Maxton both. Only I ain't gettin' back percentage."

"Wetbacks are scarce."

"You've got plenty of herd right now."

"Ah, you see? Always you know too much, friend." El Puma shook his head. "Devious. Spying on partners."

"You're takin' it up to Carraway at Bailey."

"Of course."

"And for Maxton, you have — other merchandise."

"Now, now. Do not be too devious. If you mean do I have drugs, by all means say so, friend."

"I say so. And I say Maxton's gone bad on us."

"Really, old chap? Gone bad?"

"He's ambitious."

"Caesar was an ambitious man," said El Puma. "Truly, friend, I have some ambitions also."

"Come off it," said Barty rudely. "You're after the money. That pose of yours don't go down with me."

"Really?" El Puma blew smoke through his nose. "You think my country could not do worse?"

"Could it?"

"Has done, matter of fact. Will do again. Nature of my poor country to do badly with its leaders. At least I learn. I do business, correct? I no longer raid, I trade. Mexico must get along with the giant to the north, oh, my yes indeed. But I need capital, friend. Cash."

"H'mmm. And you will sell wetbacks to Carraway. And drugs to Maxton."

"Why, of course."

There was a silence. Barty looked at El Puma with his amber eyes and suddenly seemed far more the cat than the sleek Mexican.

El Puma said uneasily, "By your permission, of course, is what I mean."

"Man like Maxton, he comes west, thinks we're all dumb yokels. 'Heckers,' I believe he calls us. He gets help from us to start things. He gets very big. He wants to ditch us."

"Us, my dear Colonel? Not us. You."

"I see. You wish to cut loose from me."

El Puma thought for a moment. "I did not say that. But Maxton directs his rebellion against you. Right?"

"You know you can't get through to Bailey without me," said Barty. "Why quibble? Just tell me how you stand. With Maxton or with me."

"Why, friend, I am with you. But how may I cope with Maxton, really? My poor herders and me against a whole townful of toughs?"

"I sent a man up there. Logan." The eyes were hooded, now. "He'll be looking after Maxton. I want my share of everything and I want you to know it and I want you to see that I get it."

"Logan?"

"Yeah. You missed him in Mexico, I hear. Kinda hurt your people a bit, didn't he?"

"Logan is your spy?"

Barty shook his head. "Logan is a United States Government man. But the government won't protect him because he's undercover, a spy, sort of."

"Logan," repeated El Puma. "I may have him?"

"If it comes out that way," agreed Barty. "He'll be after Maxton. Might be he gets Maxton. If you're around, you get Logan. I'll have another man there. Just play it the way the cards fall. But remember, I want the money, my share, every dollar. You'll never get back to Mexico without reportin' here first."

"Indeed," said El Puma. "Righto. Pip-pip, friend, and all that."

He went out, closing the door gently behind him.

Ambrose came from his place of concealment. The Colonel closed the desk drawer, wiped damp hands on a white kerchief. The brothers sat and stared at each other.

Then Ambrose said, "We ain't goin' to blow it. Not us, brother. We came too far to blow it now."

The corpse in Dinty Magin's back room was stretched on a cooling board, the limbs tied securely to offset rigor mortis, pennies upon the eyelids, ice packed up tight beneath all. Candles burned at head and feet, providing the only illumination for those who sat and watched.

There were four of them, Dinty himself, Dr. Sutton, Rose Maguire and Anne Morgan. The latter smoked a cigar and worked her hands together in her ample lap.

"They're going to dump me, I tell you," she said. "It's just a question of when and how. No use trying to get out of town, I couldn't make it."

Dr. Sutton said, "Don't keep repeating it. I'm too tired to think. This is too much."

"It's the name of the game," Rose Maguire said. "If you're around Maxton you get killed, sooner or later."

"The man's loco," said Dinty.

"Not so long as he conceals his dead,"

Sutton replied. "What about this fellow Logan?"

"Dan's all right," said Dinty. "When he finds out the whole story he might even do somethin'."

"Like what?" demanded Anne Morgan.

"Kill Maxton?" jeered Sutton.

Dinty Magin said, "If Dan Logan made up his mind to kill Maxton and had a good reason, he'd do it."

"Then give him a reason!" cried Rose. "Tell him all you know. All we can put together. Dan can't settle down here while Maxton's running things, you know that."

Dinty said, "I tried to tell him. I . . . I just ain't got the sand. If Maxton ever found out. . . ."

"You bury them. You're close to it. Rose is right. Sooner or later . . . it'll be you."

Dinty Magin said, "I druther it be later."

"A fine lot we are," Sutton said. "Among us, we know enough to have Maxton hanged higher than Hamman. So we sit here and moan about how frightened we are, knowing that our lives are not our own, that we either take orders or get ourselves murdered. We're watched day and night. It's possible that Maxton knows we are here right now, despite all our precautions."

"He knows," said Rose. "He thinks we're

having a wake." She fumbled and produced a bottle from beneath her wide skirt. "I forgot. I brought this along."

Dinty went to a cabinet on the wall and produced tumblers. Rose poured for each of them, She held her own glass in her hand, the drug was wearing off, she looked worn and ancient.

"Hell of a thing," she repeated. "Sooner or later, he gets us all."

"There I was," said Anne Morgan, "the only lady drummer in the West, making a living selling cigars. And then he dangled all that money in front of my eyes."

Rose laughed on a harsh note. "There I was, an honest whore and he set me up in his fancy apartment."

Sutton winced. "Rose, don't talk like that."

Magin suddenly put a finger to his lips, turning ashen white. They all froze for a moment, then Rose laughed again and lifted her drink.

"Well, Ford wasn't anything, come right down to it. But here's to his immortal soul."

"Amen," said Sutton.

They could hear soft footsteps now. Sutton pulled himself together. Anne Morgan stood up, downing her drink, holding out the glass for another.

Magin complained, "You're keepin' me

up with your palaverin'," making motions to them to keep up the chatter.

The door opened without ceremony as Rose spoke again, "A man's entitled to a small wake. He was Irish, you know."

Maxton walked into the room. Tanner was close behind him. They stood a moment, peering into the candlelight.

Dinty Magin said, "Why, Simon, what you doin' here at this hour? Come on in, just in time for a drink."

Maxton came closer, walked to the corpse, stared down at Ford's waxen, sunken features. Tanner stood at the door, expressionless, silent. There was silence for a moment, then Sutton cleared his throat.

"Well, I must be going. One of the Sanchez women is expecting any minute."

Maxton grinned as the doctor departed. "Damn near caught his coattails in the door. Now I wonder why Doc is so scarey?"

Rose said, "He's a very nervous man."

"You'd say that." Maxton turned his flat gaze upon her. "Why don't you make an honest man of him, Rose? But before you do that, there's customers askin' for you. Better get back to work."

She drained her glass. She got up and deliberately walked past Maxton and to the side of the dead man. She stood a moment, her head bowed, then turned and walked out of the room.

Maxton said to Anne, "You sure you gave me everything I ordered today?"

"Certainly I gave it to you."

"I ain't so sure." He turned on Magin. "I ain't so sure about anything. That Logan, he's a nosey Parker. What about him?"

"How should I know? He was a kid when he left here."

"Find out about him," said Maxton. "Otherwise you could be workin' over your own corpus."

Tanner preceded Maxton, hand on gun. The door slammed behind them. The candles guttered and Magin shivered.

"You know what that meant?" he whispered.

"The death sentence." Anne Morgan poured whiskey, spilling a little. "You better watch out. I knew I had it. Now you got it. He'll kill us all."

"What coulda got into him?"

"He's moving up," said the woman. "Don't you see that? When they move up, they clear out the back trail."

"Somethin' went wrong. You expect he was standin' out there listenin' to us?"

"It don't matter," she said. "Something went wrong, all right. He's turning against

. . . well, against the people who supply him. You wouldn't know about them."

"I don't want to know," groaned Magin.

"Did you hold out on him, Annie?"

She fumbled under her ample skirt and came up with two small canisters. "You bet I did. If I was to get out of this, I wanted a stake. Now what good are they?"

"Heroin?"

"It ain't face powder."

Magin said, "You better get rid of it."

"Where? I want it where I can pick it up again if a miracle happens."

Magin said, "I don't want it around here!" Then he said, "Wait a minute!"

His eyes went to the body. There was a pine coffin standing up in the corner. She swallowed her drink.

"Got to put him in the box any old how," said Magin. "He'll keep until we plant him in the mornin'."

"How'm I ever goin' to get it back?" She clutched the containers to her bosom.

"The German boys do like I say," he answered. "They dig shallow if I say. They dig 'em up if I say."

She said, "Oh, my God, I never laid out a stiff before."

She put the cannisters on a shelf and the two of them advanced upon the corpse.

Dan Logan entered the restaurant of Perdita Rugelo and saw the engaged couple in a corner. They waved to him and he joined them. Mel sat four square, not rising as Susan smiled, interrupting her meal.

"You're late. We expected you earlier," Mel said.

"I was delayed."

"Well, tell me, why'd you come back, Dan?"

"Everybody comes home, sooner or later." He spoke to Consuelo in Spanish, ordering a steak and rice and tomatoes. "Thought you might sell me some cows, but I see you have only your seed herd. Fine stock you have there."

"You bet it's fine. It's the best." Mel levelled the fork at Logan. "How about sellin' Rockin' Chair to me?"

Susan said, "Mel! Not at table."

Logan said, "You didn't want to buy Rocking Chair this morning. How come?"

"I thought about it. It's all got to be one. It's the only way. I'll give you a good price."

"You can afford it. You're foreclosing on Cross B. But why do you want all that land? You're running a small herd. Why do you need it?"

"Just say you'll sell," the heavy voice went on as though Logan had not spoken. "I'm a businessman."

"Pasquale was real anxious to keep me off the north section. I hear tell about a dam. Suppose you tell me about that."

"I ain't sayin' about anything. Exceptin' how much do you want for Rockin' Chair?"

"A man doesn't sell his home offhand," Logan said. "Why, we were all kids together here. This is where we all belong. Susan?"

"I'm sorry, Dan. Mel shouldn't bring it up here and now. But you can see we do need Rocking Chair."

"At the courthouse I learned a few things," Logan said. "Maxton has been buying up the small pieces in the valley. What are you going to do, build another town like Bailey? Fill it with outlanders who live by taking in each other's laundry? What's the plan?"

"Never you mind," Carraway repeated. "Name your price."

"You don't run cattle. The mines are played out. You certainly aren't farmers. I just don't understand."

Carraway shook his head like a baited bull. "No use for you to ask. I just want to buy you out. It's as simple as that."

"You can see that it makes a big, wonderful ranchero," said Susan. "We'll take care of father. The new house will be big enough for a hundred guests. We have great plans, Dan, believe me."

"But how and why?"

"That's for me to know and you to find out," Carraway said. "Name your price."

"Did you have a figure in mind?"

Mel said, too quickly, "Ten thousand dollars."

Susan said, "You can buy a fine layout for ten thousand. Mel can advise you. Mel knows."

"Yes, Mel must know." It was too much money for a broken down ranch house and acreage in the valley. Logan went on, "And he must want me long gone. Tell me, Mel, what happens if I don't sell?"

"You will." Mel actually smirked at him, nodding. "You always had horse sense, Dan. You know how things are. We need Rockin' Chair."

"You mean that you and Susan need it? Or you and Maxton?"

"All of us. Simon's a smart man."

"I'll have to think it over." Logan sliced off a piece of the meat, saw that it was juicy and tender, tasted it. "I wish they wouldn't cook their meat in oil. But it's good beef. Yours, Mel?"

"How would I know?" said Carraway carelessly. "Dan, don't think too long about sellin', huh?"

"No, Mel, I won't take much time to decide about selling to you."

"Good. I'll give you a bank draft right this minute if you say so." Mel grinned, showing large white teeth. "I know you picked up the deed at the courthouse when you paid the taxes and got your stamps."

"The answer is . . . no." Logan forked some rice, admiring the slight touch of saffron which tinted it yellow and gave it a delicate flavor.

Mel's mouth remained open. "No?"

Susan said, "Dan, you've got to think it over."

"Matter of fact," Dan said pleasantly, "I am now thinking of picking up the mortgage on Cross B."

"You are doin' what?" demanded Carraway, his face red.

"I'll check that out," said Logan. "Seems to me Ed would take a new lease on life if he didn't have a mortgage hanging over him. Bring in some cattle, horses, put Cross B together with Rocking Chair — where would you be then, Mel?"

"You ain't got the money! That'd take a fortune!"

"Oh, we won't worry about that," said Logan. "It's a good idea. It's an idea I'll be thinking about. You and Maxton, you don't need land. You've got the town. Or, at least, Maxton has. Seems to me he's better off than you. Or do you partner him in the drug traffic?"

Susan was rigid, staring at Logan. Across the table Carraway choked. Logan kept right on eating his meal.

Susan said, "Dan, you're joking. Besides, you can't buy the mortgage, the bank won't sell."

"Oh, I'll give Ed the money as a gift." He held her gaze for a moment. "You see, I'm very fond of Ed."

She dropped her eyes, then looked at Mel, nonplussed. "Talk to him, Mel."

Carraway said, "Drug traffic? Drugs? You're loco, Dan, plain loco."

"In that case, I pass," said Logan. "You want to bet Maxton's not trafficking in drugs?"

"I'm in with Simon on land. I believe in land," roared Carraway. "We bring in cattle, fatten it, sell it. A herd is on its way right now from down south." He shut his mouth tight, flustered. "From . . . out yonder. I need grazin' grounds for it. I want Rockin' Chair."

"You were always like that, Mel," said Logan. "When you were a kid you hollered to the skies if you wanted something. You didn't always get it, but you sure put up a holler."

"I'll get it! I get what I want."

Susan said sharply, "Mel! You're talking to an old friend. Dan isn't going to fight you. He has a right to his opinions. When he is here longer, he'll realize that . . . that he's wrong."

"You mean you'll talk to your father?" Logan asked. "Tell him it's all for the best? That Mel is going to take care of you and the ranch'll be yours some day in any case?"

"It's the truth," Mel said, almost shouting. "Friend? You ain't a friend, Dan Logan. I can see right here and now, you ain't a friend."

Logan chewed, swallowed. He rather regretted laying Mel wide open in this manner, but he had a job to do and it was necessary to make Susan see what lay before her, so that she might make a clear choice. "I am friend to Ed Badger," he told them. "And to Perdita Rugelo. Who else am I friend to? The wind from the Mogollons will tell, perhaps. Or the stench from a grave. You pays your money and you makes your bets, Mel. And please . . . don't holler on me, Mel. I never liked people to holler on me, remember?"

Carraway began to bellow, stopped. Susan's hand was on his arm, her eyes were pleading. He swallowed and said, "All right, Susan. All right."

"Drug traffic," said Logan distinctly. "A nasty thing. Now if you tell Maxton I said that . . . he might try and get me killed. You go ahead and do what's right, Mel. Maybe you'd better ask the wind from the mountains about it."

Susan said, "We'd best be going, now."

Logan arose, bowing. She stared at him and he saw the quick intelligence in her eyes. Mel was actually reeling with anger and also with worriment mingled with horrified belief. Logan had opened his eyes in one short sentence, he thought. Maybe Mel had suspected about the drug traffic but he had never allowed himself to realize the truth. Now everything was falling into place, because stupid as he was, he could not have helped noticing some of the facets of Maxton's operations.

Susan said, "We'll talk again."

"Why, of course. Friends, as you say."

Carraway lunged for the door. She had to quicken her steps to come even with him and then he failed to hold open the door, passing through it ahead of her.

Yet Mel Carraway was not a crook, Logan thought, resuming his meal. He was too clumsy to be a successful thief. His estimation of himself had always been too high, and therein lay his real, inner weakness. It was not beyond imagination that he would now go to Maxton and challenge him, in which case Mel would be rendered dead. Or more likely, Mel would think it over, play it up close to his vest and await developments.

Cattle coming in from the south, Logan went on in his mind. Wetbacks, no question about it. Mel's odd stammer when he spoke too hastily of them indicated it. It was common practice in the southwest to buy from Mexican rustlers who would rebrand a herd and drive them north and sell them cheap, no questions asked. All the big men of the old days of the trails had prospered by this method. But rails had changed all that and Dodge City was quiet as a church village and getting quieter and Fort Worth was no longer the Cowboy Capital.

No, there was something odd and out of key about the herd coming from the south. Logan wished he had a man to send down along the trail and check it out for him. He would have to get off a message by the next stage. Colonel Barty should know what he had learned — or guessed — thus far. It might be an idea to send Ambrose on the scout.

When he was ready he arose and went into the kitchen. Mama Rugelo was sitting on a chair in a far corner. He went to her, openly paying her for the meal. She spoke just above a whisper.

"They watch from the alley. Senor Maxton, he is aroused. There are many things happening in the town. The lady drummer is part of it. Look out for Tanner, Sunny and the Apache called Buffalo and the Negro named Mose Johnson. If they take your money, what can you do?"

"Gracias, Senora," Logan said and touched her shoulder with a gentle finger. "The rice is wonderful. I am fond of the yellow rice."

"As always," she said aloud. "God be with you."

He went out into the alley, strolling as though without a care in the world. There was the sound of action from Maxton's Palace Bar.

There were many patrons. The bar was lined, the roulette table was crowded, the faro layout was getting a play. Logan's glance swept down to the boots of the men in the place. Not one was mudstained, few were high-heeled, most were highly polished. Nobody worked but all seemed to have gambling money.

Maxton, who was there, followed him to the bar. The huge bartender's smile was wide but without humor. Tanner stood at the far end of the mahogany, a glass of beer in front of him. The Apache swamper known as Buffalo fumbled with his broom and dust pan and Logan could see the butt of a revolver in his side pocket. Mose Johnson was across the room, a shotgun at his side. Maxton gestured and Sunny brought out a bottle with a special label. The liquor was very good, Logan found.

"You scared of my tables?" Maxton's voice had a strong undercurrent of anger in it. He smiled, but he was aroused, on edge.

Logan said, "I'm on record about playing. You trying to scare me into it?"

There was a moment of silence as the tinhorns and the workingmen and the gunslingers and the bartender and the swamper and the lookout all concentrated their attention upon the two men at the bar. Logan eased around, his right hand free.

Maxton said, "Nobody has to play my games. But when a gambler refuses, it looks like he might be meaning that they ain't honest."

"Oh, come off it," Logan said, laughing. "You're not serious, are you, Maxton?"

The moment hung in delicate balance. Then Maxton laughed shortly and said, "I'm foolin', of course. Man does as he pleases. This is Liberty Hall."

There was a small stir at the far end of the place. A flight of winding stairs led upward to a balcony off which were several doors. Down the steps came Dora Bell, wearing a very tight scarlet dress and five inch spike heels. Her hair was piled atop her head and she wore rouge and something red on her lips. Behind her came Rose Maguire, slouching, hips swaying, also wearing heavy makeup. Beneath the stairs a piano began playing "Buffalo Gals," and the Apache swamper simpered and capered. The strain was broken, Logan realized.

Dora went to a faro table at one side and apart from the others and removed a baize cover. Rose went to the piano and began to sing in a whiskey voice. Men stirred along the length of the bar.

Dora Bell was laying out the game. Rose's voice was on key but too hoarse. "Those three that tried to hold me up. Who were they?"

"How should I know?" Maxton drank

again. His eyes were bloodshot. "Cutpusses. Thugs."

"I heard they came up from the south," Logan said.

"Who told you that?"

"I don't know," said Logan, purposely evasive. "Just heard it around."

"I wouldn't know," said Maxton. "People shoot off their bazoos."

"Someone got a herd coming up from the south? I want to buy some cattle, you know," pursued Logan.

"I ain't in the cattle business," said Maxton, showing annoyance. "I got my own business."

"Well, you want to discount the mortgage on Ed Badger's property?" asked Logan innocently.

Now Maxton turned and stared, black-visaged. "You got some nerve, ain't you? Tryin' to discount a sound mortgage? Buttin' in on your own friend's deal for Cross B ranch? What the hell is with you, Logan? I thought you were legit."

Logan smiled. "Why, I figure to be as legitimate as the next man. I'm a businessman in my own way, just like Mel and like you."

"It sounds like you're askin' for trouble."

"Come now, you're not telling me that

you're completely honest, Maxton. For instance — your wheel is rigged." Logan's voice did not change, he did not move a muscle, the smile remained on his face. He was overheard by at least a half dozen men, and by Dora Bell.

The men reacted as would be expected. Sunny reached for a sawed-off shotgun beneath the bar. Tanner stared as though he did not believe his ears. Three men hastily removed themselves from the vicinity. Buffalo, the Apache swamper, slid over to Mose Johnson, whispered to him.

Simon Maxton began to swell alarmingly, like a frog.

At the roulette wheel, however, only one man reacted, when Dandy Blewitt stepped back, his odd, egglike eyes rolling in his head, silver dollars in his hand. The croupier, a small man with large ears and a squint, stood with open mouth, crowding close to the table, which was covered by a cloth which hung low about its edges, very neat and clean beneath the layout of numbers and odds.

Maxton found speech. "Are you tryin' to get yourself killed?"

Now everyone's attention was on the two men. Dora Bell slid money into a drawer beneath the faro table, hesitated, took it out and put it into a small chamois bag, which she dropped into the front of her medium lowcut dress, then moved without haste to a spot near the piano. Rose Maguire asked a question with her eyebrows and Dora answered with a flick of her wrist and both women poised as for flight, like birds on the edge of a storm.

Logan moved. His speed of foot and hand was such that he had gained the roulette wheel and gently pushed the little croupier from his place before anyone realized what he was doing. He carefully removed the cloth, which had concealed the croupier's knees. He showed a lever, sat on the stool, spun the wheel and said, "Call your number, men. Any number."

Dandy Blewitt said, "I been playin' 36 red."

Logan set his knee against the wheel. The little ball fell into 36 red.

Maxton was, for once, speechless. The silence in the saloon was profound.

Logan got up and went back to the bar alongside the owner. He said calmly, "If I were you, I'd fire the man who installed that. Without your knowledge, of course. No good businessman would bother to cheat at roulette. The house percentage is big enough. I expect your croupier was knocking down the difference."

The little man moaned and ran out the side door.

"Barela!" he bellowed. "Get that Frenchy. Stick him in the pokey, you unnastand? Get him!"

Dandy Blewitt came to the bar, owlishly regarding Logan. "How'd you know, Dan?"

"The knee action. You watch them." Logan was watching Dora Bell. He thought he could detect the shadow of a smile on the pert features as she toyed with the faro case, but her eyes were brooding and worried. Rose Maguire could not conceal her wonderment and satisfaction.

Dandy whined, "Simon, I lost eight dollars tonight on that wheel. You think that's fair?"

Swallowing, Maxton pulled out a ten dollar gold piece and flung it down on the bar. "Here, take back your lousy money."

"Oh, no," said Dandy. "Take it off my bill, that's all, Simon. That's all I ask."

Maxton grunted, "Set 'em up, Sunny," and pushed the coin towards Logan. "You got somethin' comin' for tippin' me off, mister."

"Anyone can spin a wheel," said Logan. "Rose is a local lady, why not Rose?"

She flushed but came toward him, gaining

confidence with each step. He took out a gold piece of his own and flipped onto number 36. Rose hesitated only a moment, then spun the wheel.

Danny Blewitt shouted, "Thirty-six it is!"

"An honest wheel," Logan told them. He resumed his place beside Maxton. Dandy brought money and placed it before him. Logan nudged Maxton's coin away from him.

"Never gamble with another man's money," he said. "Don't thank me, Maxton. I'd advise you to keep Rose on the job. Good for the place, don't you think?"

"Yeah." Maxton was struggling with himself. It was apparent that even the loyal hangers-on had been shocked at the exposure of the crooked wheel. Open chicanery was not on his program; he was seeking political advancement. "That Frenchy, I'll have him put under that jailhouse."

Outside there was the sound of three ragged shots, unevenly spaced. Dinty's foxlike nose pointed to the door, he followed it with all possible haste. In a moment the bar was deserted excepting for Maxton, Logan, Rose and Dora and the bartender and piano player.

Logan said, "That probably accounts for Frenchy."

"Yeah," said Maxton morosely. "Barela always misses the first couple shots."

"Well, it's been interesting," Logan said. He inclined his head toward the bar's occupants. "Anytime I can help, call me."

He walked out the side door, not losing sight of Maxton. He felt a bit sick, knowing that Frenchy, a man he had never seen before, was a victim of his play, knowing that the croupier was innocent of rigging the wheel, that Maxton could not be ignorant of its crookedness, knowing that he, Logan, had signed the man's death warrant. None of them were any good, he tried to remind himself, none of them deserved more than death in the dusty street. It didn't make him feel any better.

He went up to his room and bolted the door. His mouth was dry and he knew that he needed sleep and wondered if it would come to him that night.

Down the hall from Logan's room Anne Morgan was trying to drink herself to sleep and failing, as she always had failed. Liquor was her weakness and she well knew how it affected her but could not prevent herself from soaking in it. She had gone through most of the phases. She had been scared, then boastful, then she had dragged herself to her hotel room and another bottle and now she was wallowing in maudlin self pity.

It was not her fault, she sobbed into her pillow, that she had been born . . . well, plain. Her sister was lovely and her brother the handsomest young man in Philadelphia when she was growing up. Her father, widowed, the tobacconist and cigar maker, drank too much and delighted in poking fun at her, comparing her unfavorably to the others. And when Tom was killed in the last year of the war, the old man had turned bitter. Sister Mabel had been driven from home and into a whorehouse. Anne had meekly suffered the insults and beatings and had learned to make cigars. And to smoke them.

Her money gone, she had fallen in with a salesman for tobacco. When she got the idea of traveling for the tobacco company she deliberately got the salesman fired for stealing samples, crept away from their meager lodgings in the night and took the train to St. Louis.

Barty had picked her up in El Paso on one of her escapades. He had paid off her losses, bailed her out of a bad spot. He had learned of her disinterest in bed, then had conceived the notion of making a messenger of her. He had the sample case built, with its secret compartment and had taught her the tricks of the trade. She had smuggled diamonds, dope, anything he trafficked in, and he had paid off, so that money no longer was a problem, even considering her excesses. Then this bully boy Simon Maxton had destroyed her. Just when she had reached a safe place he had interfered with threats. He was a crook and double crosser of the first water, she repeated to herself.

Despite the hour, she could not remain quiet in her room. She jammed a felt hat on her head, draped a cloak about her broad shoulders and got out of the door, forgetting to lock it. Her shoulder brushed the door of the room down the hall where Logan slept, but she managed not to stumble on the stairs.

There was no one on the streets. Everything was closed down, even Maxton's Palace Bar, but there was a light upstairs and she knew Rose had a room at the back on the second floor. Rose might have a bottle, too; she usually did have one.

Anne Morgan trudged through the dust, crossing over toward Maxton's and never saw Buffalo. The Apache had been waiting in the shadow of the restaurant, hunkered down, patient as the rocks of his native mountain country, not watching anyone in particular, merely maintaining surveillance of the town while the others held a meeting in the room above the saloon.

She was on the stairs, heading for Rose's room, when Buffalo caught her elbow in a grip like death. She tried to yell, but he struck her across the mouth, stunning her, dragging her. A door opened, light struck into the hall and then she was thrown into the presence of Maxton, Sunny, Tanner and Mose Johnson as Buffalo barred retreat and the door closed with a resounding thud.

Maxton said, "Why, Annie, you should be in bed at this hour."

"To be killed?" she wept. "I know. I know you're going to kill me."

Maxton's brows went up. He looked at the others, shrugged. "You drink too much, Annie. And when you drink you get noisy. That's bad."

"Damn you, Simon Maxton, damn you to hell. Damn you all, damn your eyes. If you didn't kill me, I'd get you. The Colonel will get you. Somebody will get you!"

Maxton said, "We want to know some things about the Colonel, you see, Annie. And about Ambrose, his man. Just any little thing you know. Sit down, Annie. We'll gab."

Buffalo slammed a chair against her knees and all the false strength drained out of her and she buried her head and sobbed and sobbed.

Maxton and the others waited.

Chapter Eight

A knock on the door brought Logan out of his sleep. He grabbed for the gun beside him, struggling awake, winding the sheet around him, staggering to stand beside the door, trying to dispel despair emanating from his nightmare.

"Quien es?" he asked, croaking, dry of throat.

"Let me in, quick!" It was Dora Bell.

He opened the door and she slid through, muffled in a full length cloak, hooded, only her eyes shining, different than he had seen them. He held the sheet tight, saying foolishly, "You don't belong here . . . You sure you weren't followed?"

"I'm here and I wasn't and you better get back in bed. You're turnin' blue," she said, practical as always.

The cold of the spring morning fully awakened him and he walked to the bed, managing to retain some semblance of dignity, wrapping the quilt about him. She came and perched beside him, throwing back the hood, breathing too quickly in short shallow gasps.

"Have they bothered you?" he asked.

"They sure did. They dragged Annie Morgan past my door a couple hours ago."

"A couple of hours?" He brushed the last cobweb from his mind.

"I had to wait until the coast was clear." She leaned toward him. "They beat hell out of her. Woke me up. She was beggin' them. Then she was quiet. You can't imagine how quiet it got."

"How close is your room?"

"Not close enough," she replied. "I couldn't make out what it was all about. They carried her out, all wrapped in blankets. They put her in a wagon and drove away. She was dead. I know she was dead."

"You're sure they didn't see you?"

"If they did, would I be here?"

"Annie Morgan," he said, reaching down to rub a cold ankle. "That could be part of it. Yes. Her sample case. It would be a good place for drugs."

"She could carry a piece of it," agreed the girl. "But if she was part of it, how come they kill her?"

"Any of several reasons."

"The old double cross? Simon is a great one for the old double cross. He's so crooked he meets himself comin' back. But the cigar lady — she's well known. Won't somebody be lookin' for her?"

"You've seen the country. By the time anyone missed her the birds would pluck her to bare bones."

She said, "I ought to be scared. That Buffalo, that Injun, he gives me the creeps. Like he's everywhere, snake-crawlin'."

"He's Apache."

"Yeah. Apache. Maybe I am scared. This ain't my dish of tea, this big old country."

"There's a stage tomorrow." Her dress was low cut and when she leaned toward him, staring at him, he glanced away, then was angry with himself. She was here, she was female and she liked him and trusted him. "Unless you want to stay around and see the show."

"Stay around, he says. A copper, yet. Am I crazy or somethin'?" Her New York voice was light but the fear was just beneath its surface. "I want to stay, Logan. Will they kill me if I stay?"

He said, "Who was driving the wagon that took Annie Morgan away?"

"Tanner and Sunny. They went north."

"That leaves Buffalo. And you think you weren't seen?" He reached out a hand. "Give me my pants."

She went to the chair where he had neatly

deposited his clothing. "You don't wear nightgear. Don't you want your longjohns?"

"Just give me the heap." He took the clothes and was surprisingly pleased when she turned her back while he donned them. She was gamin-like, but there was a quality in her that he had perceived from the start. He said, "It's time to make a move. Buffalo wouldn't let anybody out of there without spying. If he didn't go back to Maxton — or even if he did — you're in trouble and I'm in trouble."

"What's the deal?" The fear seemed to have evaporated, she was merely curious. "How do we operate?"

"You go out first. Pretend you are trying to move without being seen. Then either we take care of Buffalo or he takes care of us. I have a notion he didn't go back to Maxton yet. He wouldn't want to lose sight of you."

She watched him slip the derringer into its hiding place at his belt buckle, slide a knife in his sleeve and buckle his gunbelt. "You sure don't take chances. Do I start right now?"

"Right this minute, in case Buffalo gets any notion about getting to Maxton."

She cracked the door, peered out, and stepped down silently. He followed the shadow of the girl down the steps and across the deserted lobby of the hotel.

He saw the small, cloaked figure of the girl gliding along the street, casting anxious glances behind her, to each side of her. He came out of the hotel secure in the knowledge that if the Apache had picked her up he would be concentrating on the chase. He ran on swift, purposeful feet to the shadowed corner of Maxton's Palace.

Buffalo came out with a knife poised. The girl did a quick sidestep, then lowered her head and stood firm. The knife slashed toward her throat.

Logan caught the Apache's wrist. In the same motion he brought his forearm beneath Buffalo's chin, preventing an outcry. The girl crouched like a prizefighter, hands slightly apart, cloak streaming back, ready, Logan realized in amazement, to give help.

Buffalo tried an Indian trick with his left foot. Logan shifted his balance and brought the forearm into the jugular. The Apache was wiry but could not wrest loose the wrist that Logan bent inward, inch by inch. Logan snapped hard, spinning him against the wall of the saloon, leaning on the hand holding the knife.

It went in clean, between ribs, on the left side. Buffalo made one effort but lacked the breath. He jerked hard, his legs kicked.

Logan put a finger on the pulse in his neck. After a moment he knew the Indian was dead.

He pulled the girl into the alley. "Where is your room?"

"Head of the stairs. Cheez, that was a neat one, Logan."

"Never mind that. Up we go."

He admired her slim ankles, the speed and dexterity of her. They came to a door and she knew enough to edge it, wait a moment while Logan went in with his Colt in his hand.

He whispered in her ear, "Take whatever is valuable and your riding clothes. Nothing else."

She said, "I got gowns here worth a fortune!"

"They'd look fine on a corpse," he reminded her. "Move! Quick!"

It took her less than two minutes to make a small bundle and place it in a leather bag which could be easily utilized as a saddlebag. She wore the riding clothes beneath her cloak, with a felt hat pulled low. He had been watching at the door as she changed; they were very circumspect, he thought, for a pair of experienced rounders.

When they were on the street again she asked, "Now where and the hell do I go?"

"I have a friend, Ed Badger."

"The county drunk?"

"That's what they say of him. But his man, Sarge Cornwall, can be trusted to the hilt. It's either Cross B or the stage at Silver, if they let you get to Silver and on the stage."

She sighed. "How far to Cross B?"

He took her into the livery stable. Monterey was not in view. He saddled the black horse.

She asked, "Which one will I borrow?"

"You ever tried riding double?"

"It's uncomfortable."

"If they check and another horse is missing they can find it — and you."

"Well," she said, "what have I got to lose?"

He put her up behind him, on the saddle roll. She wrapped her arms about his middle. She was surprisingly strong — always surprising, he thought. They rode over back lots, taking no chances, going by the most devious route he could remember.

"Tanner and Sunny are hiding Annie Morgan somewhere in these hills," she reminded him.

"But how well can they hide her? I doubt they'll go very high or very deep. I'll have a look, after I leave you at the ranch."

They began the ascent of Mob Hill as the first small trace of pink light stretched in the eastern sky. They fell silent as they wended a precarious way on a road not much wider than the stirrups. They came to the summit and paused, looking down upon the valley.

"That's Cross B, right? The closest one?"

"That's it."

They rode down to Cross B. There Logan left Dora Bell with the colored man. "Keep her out of sight and well fed until I check in."

Logan then went into the house. He found Ed Badger without going upstairs. Snores came from the parlor.

Logan shook the drunken man by the shoulder. "Time to rise and shine, Ed."

"Who . . . what . . . ?" Badger came to his feet, his hand reaching for a gun that wasn't at his side. "Oh . . . Daniel. Just don't stand there, Daniel. Get the jug."

Logan pushed him back on the couch. "Not today. I have to talk to you."

Badger said, "You can talk but I can't listen. Got to have a snort before my ears work."

"You'll listen."

Badger snorted. "You crazy, or somethin'?"

"Maybe I am. I just killed the Apache, that nasty little snake, Buffalo."

"Nice work," said Badger. "Gimme a drink, I'll celebrate."

"There's going to be a lot of killing," Logan told him, enunciating carefully. "But first I want to set up something. I want you to take over Rocking Chair."

"Ha! Can't even hold onto Cross B! You want Mel and Susan to take over."

"I want you."

"Can't have me. I'm all gone."

"You keep saying that. I'm going into town and buy up your mortgage. That's before the killing begins. Then I'm going to deed Rocking Chair over to you in case I'm one of the victims. There's a girl in your barn, I want you to talk with her, look after her until I make it one way or the other. Maxton will murder her if he knows she's here. And I'm paying off the mortgage this morning. Now, Ed, you think it over. Just think about it."

He turned and walked out. He saw the older man grope for the jug beneath the couch and his heart sank. He went back to the barn where he mounted the buckskin and saw the girl looking at him with fear and sorrow. "Don't worry, Dora. I've been tried before. They seem to miss me a lot."

She said, "I think I'm scared, now."

"You're never scared." He leaned down

151

from the saddle and brushed her cheek with his lips. She was very soft to the touch. "Stick with it. I'll see you."

He took the high road toward town, now, riding fast on the long-legged and willing black horse. He thought about the small woman from New York. She was a rare one, unlike any other female alive, he imagined. Sometimes she seemed almost masculine, then she switched on that other side of her and bowled a man over. Well . . . nearly over. Logan had seen a good many women since Susan Badger was his girl.

He was about to ride past Rocking Chair when he saw fresh wagon tracks. He swung the buckskin and followed the trail up to the house. Tanner and Sunny had been far from subtle. He went through the house to the large closet in the dining room, where his mother had kept the dishes and other household paraphernalia. Annie Morgan was still wrapped in a blanket.

There was no wound which might cause death. He closed the dead, staring eyes. Drugs, he thought, in the end they injected her with an overdose. No blood, no noise, very nice and neat.

At that moment Paul Crown's drawl from behind him froze him to the spot. "You wanta let me look at it?"

Logan turned very slowly, hands upraised. Crown had his gun in his hand and was moving forward.

"You won't like it," Logan suggested.

Crown stopped, his mouth agape, his eyes wide. Logan rapped him on the wrist and knocked the revolver away from him. Crown didn't bat an eye; he continued to stare.

Logan said, "If you know anything about tracking or about corpses, you'll know I couldn't have killed her."

"Ugh," said Crown. "I seen the wagon come in. Then I seen you. No, you didn't do it. Ain't your style, nohow."

Logan picked up the Colt and handed it over. "It isn't often you see a woman done in this way."

"Annie Morgan, the lady drummer. Hell, I knowed her for years. Who done that to her?"

"Maxton," said Logan. "Any more questions?"

"Maxton." Crown slipped his gun back into the holster. "His bunch. Some bunch."

"Did he have you kill Ford?"

Crown sucked in his breath. "Sometimes I ain't plumb smart, you know that? I listened when Maxton told me how Ford ran the deck. Ford had taken a few dollars from me. I had a couple drinks in Maxton's place and he fed me the information. He was tellin' the truth."

"He set Ford up."

"How 'bout that? He led me to it. I did the rest. The poor goddam tinhorn."

"Carraway doesn't know anything about Maxton's business excepting what he's supposed to know?"

"Carraway don't know doodley-squat," Crown said firmly. "He don't know his hiney from his off elbow. Exceptin' he knows how to make money and in my book that ain't any great shucks." Crown shivered, then said, "I'm hired to Carraway. He plumb needs a nurse. But when the times comes, will you gimme a chance? I don't often drop my gun."

"I'll need you," said Logan. "You don't know what it means to me to have the offer."

"I know what it means to me," said Crown. "I liked old Annie."

On the cattle trail south of Bailey a herd of nearly a thousand wetback long-horns grazed. At the chuck wagon Miguel de Santa Ferra drank hot, black coffee and talked with Tomas, known as The Spider.

"They grow fat. They will bring a good

price," said the lieutenant, speaking in Spanish.

"Yes," responded El Puma in kind. "They bring money from the fool, the Senor Carraway."

"But more dinero from the Senor Maxton, no?"

"From the Senor Maxton, yes."

"And for the Colonel Barty?"

El Puma made a slicing motion across his throat. "His share is too great, no? You fully understand?"

"I understand, jefe. I understand also from the Senor Logan. It is he whom I must see firmly secured by us."

"No," said El Puma sharply. "No chances taken, you must be certain. This one, he is the most dangerous."

"Gorda, he wants Senor Logan beneath his small knife."

"Gorda will end where the others ended. And you, my fine friend, you will end there also, a hole in the earth if you tamper with my plans. If Logan gets within range, we kill him. No nonsense with knives. Bullets, and quick!"

"Then it must be so," said Tomas resignedly. "It is of a deep shame, however."

"Better shame than dead," El Puma told him.

There were a dozen heavily armed men around the trail encampment. Gorda moved among them, always alert. El Puma sipped the coffee, hugely satisfied with himself. These were recruits from the hills, bad men all. They would fight for the love of it, for tortillas and beans. The amount he paid them bound them to him with chains.

It would be the last journey. There were more men in the mountains. He had received good news from the capital, there was more unrest than usual in the government. With the money he would take from Bailey, the money from Maxton and the money from Carraway, and whatever he could steal from the bank, the rest of the town, he would set up headquarters and begin planning for his march to glory.

He smiled, a happy, carefree man, a soldier of fortune whose luck had at last turned, he thought.

On a high hill to the east of the cattle herd Colonel Barty lowered his field glasses and remarked, "Might not be the biggest on the trail. But it's the most valuable."

"El Puma's got twice the men he needs," said Ambrose. "He's pullin' an extra wagon, too. Full of ammunition and ready to tote off loot, I'd guess."

Barty said, "We better make tracks. Got to beat 'em into town."

"Do we?" Ambrose frowned. "Where at you figurin' to put up? You think we'll be welcome?"

"Sent Logan in, didn't we?" Barty shrugged. "He's our man. Up to him to take care of us. Once we warn him about El Puma, he'll know what to do."

"You sure have got a nerve," said Ambrose admiringly. "Use a man for cover, then kill him."

"You'll kill him," disclaimed Barty. "Not me. I may have to kill El Puma or Maxton, if Logan don't beat us to it. If I can get them to sit down across a table."

"They won't want to sit down," Ambrose warned him. "They don't expect us nohow."

"Element of surprise. Like in a war." Barty brushed a hand through his whiskers. "Logan's the key. If he does what I think, our job'll be collecting the money, saving Bailey from looting, taking over the ranch property. It's time to move out of El Paso, leave the government to its own devices. You got to know timing, Ambrose. Most important. Let us ride."

They rode toward Bailey, picking up speed, leaving the herd behind on the trail.

■ ■ ■ ■

Sunny and Tanner carried the body of Buffalo up the stairs and into the room at the end of the hall, from where they had earlier removed Annie Morgan. Maxton came, rubbing his eyes, disbelieving.

"He done himself in? Buffalo? You're out of your foolish, bleedin' heads."

"His hand was on the knife," Sunny said. "Stuck right in the ribs where it would do the most good."

Maxton said, "Why should he do it? Tell me that."

"I wouldn't know," said Sunny. "I never did know nothin' about the Apache bastard. He was too sneaky for me."

"He was the best man for this country we had," Maxton shouted. "What the hell's the matter with you guys? Don't you know we need a westerner, a real one?"

"Damn Injun," grunted Tanner. "Never trusted him. Prob'ly got high on somethin' and went crazy."

"And you're supposed to be brainy birds," said Maxton. "Have you checked everybody?"

"We just got here. There's no one here but the dames and us."

Maxton said, "Get the women in here."

He paced the floor, staring again and again at the dead Apache, trying to figure out how the knife had been inserted. He bent to look at the throat, but there were no visible marks on the leathery, dark skin. Someone, he knew, had forced that blade into Buffalo's heart. It had to be that way. It didn't make sense any other way.

Sunny came back, dragging Rose. Her eyes were puffed and she was obviously waking from drugged slumber. But Maxton leaped upon her and slammed her down on the floor alongside the corpse, demanding information.

She did not seem to comprehend. "Buffalo? Stabbed? Who could get . . . who could come near him?" She looked up at Maxton, her mouth slack. "Nobody could get that close to Buffalo."

Maxton toed her aside. "Take her back, Sunny. Where's that Dora Bell?"

Tanner entered and said, "She ain't in the building. Her clothes is all there exceptin' her pants — you know the outfit. Mebbe she went for a midnight ride."

"Yeah, she's sure nuts about horses," said Sunny. "Never did see a dame from New York go for horses like her."

Maxton said, "The livery stable.

Monterey. Check with him. Don't take any manure from him; I pay him for what he knows."

Sunny went without ceremony. Tanner took Rose away, supporting her as she rubber-legged on uncertain feet.

He went over what he had learned from Annie Morgan when she had finally been unable to hold back under the torture. Doc Sutton and Dinty Magin and maybe Rose. They didn't count, they could be disposed of one at a time. They were nothing and they had nobody to back them. None could have handled Buffalo, because Buffalo had heard Annie squeal and knew about them.

"Okay," said Maxton. "Take Buffalo downstairs and be ready to bury him."

He wondered about Logan. He walked until he almost fell asleep on his feet, wondering about Logan.

CHAPTER NINE

It was midmorning and Logan was enjoying a combination breakfast and lunch, chile relano with enchiladas stuffed with cheese from goat's milk. Maxton entered by the rear door, stopped when he saw that his special table was occupied, scowling.

Logan said brightly, "Thought you

160

wouldn't mind, since I have some business to talk over with you."

Maxton seated himself heavily, showing the effects of a hectic night, his low brow still furrowed. "What kinda business?"

"Well, I rode out to Cross B this morning early," said Logan.

Maxton interrupted, "What was you doin' out at that hour is what I wanta know?"

Logan smiled. "You do keep track of people, don't you? Why, I had to talk with Ed Badger, of course." He reached into his breast pocket and dropped a sheaf of bank notes before Maxton. "His mortgage. I'm picking it up."

Maxton growled, "You can't do that. It's already spoke for."

"You refuse to take my money?" Logan's eyebrows shot up. "Cash? When the note's not due yet?"

"I tell you it's been asked for." Maxton was a bit confused. "What you want of that run-down place?"

"This country needs building up," said Logan earnestly. "I figure to combine my ranch with Cross B, stock them with good cattle. You don't think it's a good notion?"

"It's a lousy idea," muttered Maxton. He poked at the notes with a thick finger. "You can't come in here and upset deals like this."

Logan said injuredly, "Maxton, I'm disappointed in you. I thought you were a businessman. Money talks to a smart businessman. And if you don't take my money, what will they think at the capital? The legislature wouldn't think it was honest, straightforward, legal, would it?"

Maxton said, "Look, your own friend wants that place. He's goin' to marry Badger's daughter. What kind of guy are you to butt in?"

"A businessman," said Logan blandly. "I need someone to help run my place. Ed Badger is my man."

"We'll go over to the bank," said Maxton finally. "It's too bad for Carraway. But business is business, right?"

"Right," said Logan. "Try this dish, it's delicious. Senora Rugelo makes it to the king's taste."

Maxton ordered. The meal was concluded with no more than desultory conversation. Maxton's mind was going around and around, Logan thought, not arriving anywhere in particular at the moment. They had disposed of Buffalo without consulting Dinty Magin, he had learned. They had to be somewhat confused. If he could keep them off balance until the herd came in . . . but he couldn't think any further than that.

El Puma was another matter. He wondered if Ambrose would show up.

They left the restaurant and went into the bank. There were two young men behind the cages and an ancient rifleman on a balcony overlooking the premises. Maxton gestured at the latter. They went into a private office and Maxton worked the combination of the old safe which Logan remembered from the days of his youth. The mortgage deed was in order. Logan read it through, looked for a cuspidor, lighted a match and burned the document.

"Now Cross B belongs to Ed Badger," he said.

"I thought it belonged to you."

"Oh, no," said he carelessly. "Ed's an old friend. We're just combining the two spreads, that's all."

"But he can't run nothin'! He's a drunk! His own daughter wouldn't trust him."

Logan said, "Strange, isn't it? I trust him."

Maxton said, "I just don't understand you, unless you got more money than you know what to do with."

"I have enough," lied Logan. "When that herd comes in, I want a crack at buying a few head for starters."

"What herd?" Maxton was again suspicious.

"The one you told me about, remember?"

"I didn't. . . ." He broke off. Had he mentioned the herd in connection with the three holdup men in the kitchen of the Rugelo place? He couldn't remember. He needed sleep, that was it. He got up and said, "All right, Logan. It's your wagon, you pull it. Just don't take too much for granted, huh?"

"Whatever that means," said Logan agreeably. "See you later?"

He departed the bank and its new president. He went up the street to Dinty Magin's place and entered. Dr. Sutton and the carpenter-undertaker were in close conversation. They started apart as Magin said, flustered, "Oh, we was just talkin' about you, Daniel. Did you say you seen Annie?"

"Oh, yes, I saw her. She's up in the hills. Dead as a mackerel," said Logan.

"They killed her," Magin said to Sutton. "I told you. They killed her."

"They surely did," Logan agreed. "Tortured her a bit first. I'd bet she talked."

The two men went white as driven snow. Logan let them sit under it for a moment. Then he spoke.

"I just picked up Ed Badger's mortgage. We're going to work both ranches together. I'll want the town clean, though. Can't do business in a town like Bailey is now."

Dr. Sutton said deep from his chest, "Do you mean that, sir?"

"There ain't enough of us," Magin cried. He scampered to the door, peered up and down. "If Buffalo hears us, they'll kill us next."

"Buffalo is also dead," Logan told them. "He sort of impaled himself on his own knife sometime this early morning. The Bell girl is at Cross B."

Then Magin said, "But besides El Puma there's a bigwig in El Paso. He's in on it, too. We had a man, Donnelly, he was closin' in, but he got killed. Gunman named Ambrose shot him."

"Ambrose!" Logan was startled.

"Yeah. This whole thing is real mysterious, Daniel," wailed Magin. "What can we do? Just the three of us. If we could get Carraway and Paul Crown away from Maxton, mebbe. . . ."

Logan said, "Speak of the devil. Here's Mel now, and I think he's looking for me."

They went to the door. Carraway was coming from the bank, his boots throwing up spurts of dust, striding long and heavily. Susan Badger sat in the carriage across the street, her face pale. With some shock, Logan realized she must have spent the night at Lazy Dog with her fiancé.

Carraway shouted, "Dan! Dan Logan!"

He stepped out into the street and answered, "You want me, Mel?"

Behind Logan, Magin said, "Fire's comin' out of his eyes, his nose and his ears."

"He's a terrific fighter," Dr. Sutton whispered. "Use your gun, Logan."

Down the street, ambling, hat on the back of his head, came Paul Crown. It could be a setup, Logan thought, with Susan a witness. It could be, but he didn't think so.

Carraway was yelling, "You buttinsky, what the hell do you mean lifting Ed's mortgage?"

"Why, I mean business. Legitimate business," said Logan. Across the street Maxton, Sunny, Tanner and Mose Johnson were crowding to see the fracas. From farther down came Mama Rugelo, her son and daughter, Dandy Blewitt and the rest of the population of Bailey.

"You mean I aimed to steal Cross B from Ed? Why, you damn fool, he's to be my father-in-law."

"Well?"

"That ranch is for me and Susan."

"But Ed's an old friend of mine," Logan said. "You think Ed's finished. I disagree."

"You double crossin' skunk, you're just

sore because I'm marryin' your gal!" roared Carraway. "Men have been killed in this country for less!"

"Really, Mel?" Logan winked at Crown, who stood idly nearby. "I wouldn't want to be killed."

He unbuckled his gunbelt and handed it to Crown. The lanky cowboy took it and stepped out of the way. Now it was impossible for either Carraway or Crown to draw — to all intents and purposes Logan was unarmed. Crown tapped his belt, knowing of the derringer, merely shook his head and was reassured by Logan's nod.

Carraway ran to the carriage and left his gun with Susan. The girl bit her lips but offered no expostulation.

"I'm goin' to beat tar outa you," Carraway yelled. "I been wantin' to do this for years."

Logan asked quietly, "Is that why you smashed up my mother's house? Because you've been angry with me for years. Is that why, Mel?"

His guess struck home. Carraway flushed brick red. He gritted his teeth and leaped into action. He swung a polelike right arm.

Logan reached into his pocket as he ducked the punch, letting Carraway rush past him. He took out a pair of rawhide driving gloves and turned, waiting, poised on the balls of his feet. The big man came roaring again. Logan feinted, let him go past again, adjusting the gloves.

Carraway was coming again, the first rage evaporated, taking his time, confident. He shortened his punch, aiming at the body, trying to press Logan toward Magin's place and nail him to the wall.

Logan went to work. He evaded Carraway's clutch, staying on the toes of his soft leather boots. He jabbed delicately with his left. He hit Carraway four times in the right eye without a return. Then he stepped back.

Mel obliged, furious, blinking, rushing again. Logan pretended to sidestep, then came back, straight into the big guns of the larger man. He blocked, picked off a swinging hook, countered. His left went to the nose, his right dug in at the ribs, then went in again, like a hammer tapping, tapping.

Then he was away again, revolving on his right foot, toeing with his left. Carraway let out a breath and growled, "You lowdown skunk, you're scared to stand up and fight like a man."

The words were scarcely spoken when Logan went in. The left speared again and blood ran from the Carraway proboscis. The right came under and up and landed with a smack on Mel's hard jaw.

Logan poised, ducking, watching. He saw Carraway try to seize him in a bear hug, went right into it. A gasp arose from the onlookers.

Then Magin said, "I don't believe it!"

Logan had struck at the wind, his fists beating a tattoo too swift to follow. Carraway's arms dropped, his mouth flew open. Logan closed it with an uppercut.

Carraway stood with his hands down, staring, breathless. Logan danced in, put a hand against the heaving chest. He pushed, not very hard.

Carraway sat down in the dirt.

Logan suggested, "If you're satisfied, I'd as soon quit this, Mel. You might be badly hurt if we keep on."

Logan turned. Across the street Susan was glaring at him. She was dry-eyed, however. He wondered how deeply she cared for the bruised hulk of a man Crown was aiding across the street. People were dispersing now. Maxton and his crew were returning to the Palace. Mose Johnson was mumbling something about, "He's a ringer. He done larned too good, some place. Nobody but a professional knows them moves."

Logan said to Sutton, "If you're thinking about Rose Maguire, she's in danger. Maxton will be after her for what she knows.

Remember, Annie Morgan talked."

"I've got to get her out of there," said Sutton.

"That's easy, if you go and take her right now," Logan advised.

"I . . . I can't. I'm . . . no good at that sort of thing."

"Well, then, I'll go with you," Logan offered. It was the time to strike, he thought. The iron was pretty hot.

Then the door flew open and Ed Badger staggered into the room. He was as drunk as he could manage and still maneuver, Logan realized. He pointed a shaky finger and said, "You can't do it, Daniel. You can't do it to me and my daughter."

"Daniel, he's wearing his guns!" Magin said in quick and acute fear.

Logan moved close to the older man. "How did you get here, Ed?"

"None of your damn business. . . ."

Logan moved with all his speed, catching Badger by both wrists, slamming him onto a chair. "Dr. Sutton, your bag. Morphine, I think, will sober him."

The medico fumbled with his bottles and syringes, his hands shaking. Magin cowered in a corner, remembering the awesome feats of Ed Badger in his gunslinging days.

"The girl. Where's the girl?"

"Damn fool woman came along. Wouldn't stay behind like I told her." Badger's eyes were crossed, he became lachrymose. "Why'd you do it, Daniel? Couldn't believe it when Sarge told me you were buyin' the place from under my little gal. Why?"

"I haven't got time for drunk nonsense," Logan told him, furious at the untimely interruption. "Doc?"

Dr. Sutton timidly tried to pull up Badger's sleeve. With a powerful lunge, the old rancher threw Logan arm's length from him, twisting and struggling. "Nobody's goin' to stick no damn needle in me!"

Logan sighed and hit his oldest friend on the chin. Badger sagged back onto the chair. "Give him enough to keep him quiet for awhile," Logan said. "We've got to move and move fast."

Dr. Sutton managed to inject the morphine.

Logan said, "Bring that bag of yours. Follow my lead. You could get killed in the next half hour, I want you to know that."

"I understand." The doctor's hands were trembling, his eyes watered, but he followed Logan to the door.

Magin wailed, "What about me? If you get it, what becomes of me?"

"You'll be in trouble," said Logan.

He led the way across the street. They entered Maxton's Palace, stepping briskly, purposefully. The hangers-on batted their eyes, the Maxton men stayed in their positions, looking at the leader, waiting, poised. Mose Johnson muttered, "Lemme take him. I'll show him tricks o' the fancy."

Dr. Sutton strode toward the stairs. He may have been frightened, Logan thought, but he was able to conceal it from the crowd in the saloon. Logan hung an elbow on the bar and smiled at Maxton.

Sunny barred Sutton's path, asking in his odd, merry fashion, "You goin' somewhere, Doc?"

Logan said, "Got a lady upstairs not feeling good. Rose Maguire."

There was a long pause, then Maxton left the side of Mose Johnson and came to face Logan at the bar. "You interested in Rose?"

"Knew her years ago," shrugged Logan. "Have a mornin's mornin'?"

The two inches of brow furrowed again. Maxton said fretfully, "You don't seem t' unnastand, Logan. If Rose has got the fantods or somethin', she's supposed to tell me about it."

Logan lifted one shoulder. "Is that the law? If so, it's unconstitutional." He lowered his voice. "If you want to be a legitimate businessman you'd better watch these little details. Now, tell your bartender to get out of the way before there's a scandal."

"Scandal?" Bewildered, Maxton motioned to Sunny. Dr. Sutton went stiffly up the stairs. Maxton asked, "How do you figure, scandal?"

"You know what's happening to Boss Tweed in New York?"

"Sure, I know. That's why I come. . . ." He broke off.

"You have to be careful," Logan told him.

Maxton rallied. "What I wanta know, who told you Rose was sick? Was it that Dora Bell twist?"

Logan looked him in the eye. "Annie Morgan told me." He reached for his drink, watching Maxton swallow, boggle his eyes, then grab and toss off four ounces of whiskey.

"Oh. I see."

"You know Annie and Rose are friends," Logan said. "They've known each other a long time."

"I know that. I know. . . ." Maxton looked wildly around. He knew of course that Logan was lying. What he could not understand was why. He was getting a glimmer, Logan thought. It was slowly coming to him. When it hit home, there would be hell to pay.

But then, if the herd from the south was anywhere close, it was time for hell to be paid. Dr. Sutton and Dinty Magin were weak reeds upon which to lean. Maxton must be kept off balance until the time came to strike.

Tanner and Mose Johnson were moving closer. Sunny had his hand beneath the bar. Maxton swallowed hard, looked around with a sick smile.

Then there was a sound on the stairway and everyone turned. Dr. Sutton had put a blanket around Rose Maguire and was supporting her step by step down to the saloon. Her face was pale and drawn, he was stern, glaring.

"This woman should have been hospitalized before now," the doctor proclaimed. "This is outrageous."

"Hospital?" floundered Maxton. "What hospital?"

"Why, the one we are endowing over at Magin's," said Logan. "You don't keep up with the town, do you?"

"The town?" He choked again. "But . . . who started anything like a hospital?"

"A good politician knows these things," said Logan helpfully. "But I'll tell you. It really started when the tinhorn, Ford, lay there hurting. We just put in a few dollars each to help Doc get supplies and things. Your share would be . . . well, I'll leave it to you, Maxton."

"My share?"

"Whatever you want to donate. The people of the county will all be in on it, of course."

Maxton said, "Yeah. Sure. I'm all for it." He reached into his pocket, took out a sheaf of notes. Logan took them from his hand, riffled them. Maxton could only stare.

"Over a thousand. Say, that's wonderful. We'll see to it everybody learns about this," said he. "Very generous. Thanks a lot, Maxton."

He finished his drink, and walked out across the dusty street and into Magin's. He handed the money over to Sutton.

He said, "Use it for a hospital. It was an idea I had . . . Now, Rose, what about the drug traffic?"

She said, "Whatever Doc gave me, it made me awful sick for now. I'll tell you later."

Sutton said, "We'll put her in the ward. That'll be where Mr. Badger is sleeping it off. Later, we can talk."

Logan said, "That suits me. I have to find the girl, anyway."

He left them heading toward the livery

stable, knowing that the girl would have sense enough to remain out of sight. He saw Monterey in the yard, uneasy, wall-eyed, unable to take his gaze from the barn for longer than a moment. He went inside and leaned against a stall.

From the hayloft, Dora Bell called, "You want me to stay up here? My nose itches."

"Sneeze," offered Logan.

She sneezed.

Logan suddenly realized he wanted to see the girl, to watch her impish face, talk with her, listen to her odd but amusing flow of language. He shook himself, frowning. "I'll be around. The whole thing hinges on that herd from the south, I think. Just stay close and wait."

"If I don't sneeze my head off," Dora said. "Don't you take any wooden money, Logan."

"I'm a bit more frightened of lead bullets," he said as he departed.

Maxton, he thought, would be rallying his wits — and his forces. Every shortcarder and tinhorn and would be gunslinger, even stupid Santos Barela would be a part of the army. If it was possible to ride south and scout the incoming herd, he would know exactly how to act. But he did not dare leave the town at this juncture. He went toward the hotel, hoping to get time to wash up and change his clothing and also to direct Pedro Rugelo to secretly convey food to Dora.

A lanky form disengaged itself from a chair in the lobby and asked, "Are you Mr. Logan?"

He cocked an eyebrow at Ambrose and said, "Why, yes. Do I know you?"

"No, sir. But I wanted to talk to you about some cattle for sale."

Logan said, "Fine. Shall we go up to my room?"

They went up the stairs and Logan put the key in the lock and motioned to Ambrose, who drew his gun and stood to one side. Then Logan kicked the door open and ducked, kneeling, his own weapon sweeping the interior. There was no sound, no movement.

They went in and wordlessly searched every inch of the room, peering beneath the bed and in the wardrobe, then looking out the window onto the roof of the verandah. Satisfied, they faced one another, grinning.

"Good to see you, Ambrose."

"Good to see you. Thought you'd like to know that El Puma and a herd of cattle — wetbacks — is comin' in about tomorrow mornin'."

Logan said, "That's just what I wanted to know."

"Got a lil ole problem for you," Ambrose went on.

"Another problem? This country's full of 'em."

Ambrose said, "The Colonel's here."

"Barty? He came here with you?" Logan was truly surprised. "What in the hell for?"

"You can ask him. He wants to be hid out."

Logan said, "That's all I do, hide people. They'll be falling over each other. I do have a place in the livery stable which isn't overcrowded at the moment. Where is he now?"

"Outside town, north a way. He don't like waitin' too long, you know. It was a long ride."

Logan said, "All right, we'll put him on Cross B. Nobody out there, right now."

"That Badger's place?"

"Badger's in town, so is his foreman." For some reason, partially through habit, Logan went no further. "There's food out there. And corn likker, God knows, plenty of corn."

"Colonel don't drink no corn, you know that. How do we get to the place?"

Logan told him, then asked, "Are you

coming back? To Bailey, I mean?"

"You gonna need some backin'," Ambrose said. "You got anything on Maxton yet?"

"Let's talk to the Colonel," said Logan. "Then I won't have to tell it twice."

"Fine," said Ambrose. "You want to meet at Cross B?"

"I'll follow you there, after I attend to some matters," Logan promised.

He watched Ambrose lounge out of the room. He sat down and pondered. He had expected Ambrose. But what was Barty doing here? What was the huge stake which led him to place his precious person in jeopardy?

He washed, changed his shirt and went down to the lobby. Pedro was behind the desk. Logan moved close to him and spoke in lowered tone.

"Can you sneak some food to the hayloft of the livery stable?"

"Si, Senor Logan. Mama says to do what you want me to do."

"Make sure nobody sees you. The girl from Maxton's is up there. Understand?"

"I understand there is finally someone to go against Maxton," Pedro said directly. "We all understand that. We are watching — and waiting."

"Waiting for what?"

Pedro's teeth flashed. "For the moment of truth, Senor. Then you will see."

"Don't get yourselves killed," Logan warned him. "There's too many of them."

Pedro said, "We will die, if we have to, for our town, our place. If it could be like before. Oh, si, Senor, we will die, some of us. But some will live."

Logan started to protest, could not find words. He said, "Go in peace, Pedro. Feed my friend."

He went out and noticed there were several of the dark-skinned Mexican-Americans in evidence, more than he had previously seen. It wrenched at him that these innocents might move recklessly and involve themselves in what promised to be a full scale war. He went thoughtfully to the livery stable. Monterey was in the barn, his attitude one of total resignation.

Dora called, "You bring my food, Logan?"

"Didn't dare. Pedro'll slip it in." He said to Monterey, "Saddle up my black."

"Si, si," said the beleaguered livery stable owner.

He asked in Spanish, "How is it that you are employed by Maxton?"

Monterey's color deepened. "I have eight children, Senor. My wife, she is much afraid of Senor Maxton."

"But you're not afraid of him?"

"I pray to God that I fear no man," said Monterey solemnly. "Only the Lord himself."

"Just keep it in mind," Logan advised him. "And when the moment comes, perhaps you will be on the side of the Lord. Quien sabe?"

"No, but I listen," said Monterey with dignity. "I am thinking of my eight children and my wife."

Logan went inside and looked up at the hayloft. Dora's pixie countenance peered down at him.

"Hay is for horses," she said. "I'm hungry."

"Just be satisfied you're alive," he told her lightly. "Annie Morgan isn't, you know."

She shuddered. "How about Rose?"

"With Sutton and Magin but far from safe."

"Oh. Where you goin' on the horse?"

"To Cross B. El Puma's bringing the herd in tomorrow. We'll have to go to work then."

"Take it easy, now Logan. Can't do without you, remember."

She blew him a kiss. He mounted and rode out, carefully holding the black down to an easy walk. She was different from any other woman he had met. She was getting under his skin with her bravery and her cheerfulness and her good, common sense so seldom found in the other sex.

He rode out of town, turned off the road, doubled back. No one was following. He aimed the black for Cross B.

Chapter Ten

Maxton walked the floor of the office. Tanner and Mose Johnson and Sunny sat around the table smoking the cigars from Annie Morgan's sample case.

Sunny said, "I got High Pockets and Sloppy Joe and Freddy Fay keepin' the boys alive. What can happen?"

"That Logan. Why'd he say he seen Annie Morgan?"

Mose Johnson said, "You got to lemme scrag Logan."

"But he brought in money," Maxton said. "You don't unnastand. He may know somebody in the capital. He may be where he could gimme a black eye up there. I got to make a splash in Santa Fe."

"We could take the loot and move on," ventured Tanner. "Start some other place."

"No!" Maxton was definite. "I got it made here. We own this here place. We're gonna keep it. We're gonna be big people here. No coppers, our own law . . . what about that Barela?"

"He's watchin' downstairs," said Sunny.

"What about Rose?"

"Still in the joint, Magin's, with the corpuses."

"There'll be a funeral tomorrow."

"That's all right. Keep 'em busy while the herd's comin' in. Where's Carraway?"

"That's another thing," said Maxton. "Where is dumbhead? Logan beat on him and he went home to cry in his woman's lap, probably."

"It's a lot of money," Tanner said. "If we took Carraway and shipped the stuff and grabbed the bank we could set up real good some place. Like South America."

Maxton glared at him. "South America? Ain't you got no patriotism? Who wants South America?"

They puffed cigar smoke, silent for a moment. There was a knock on the door and Barela's voice said, "El Puma's people is here."

"Let 'em in," said Maxton. Then he growled, "What they doin' here tonight?"

The others took out revolvers and held them in their laps under the table as a matter of course. Maxton went to the head of the table as Gorda and Tomas came into the room, Barela waiting behind them.

Maxton said, "Downstairs, Barela, and keep your eyes open. If Logan shows, I wanta see him."

"Okay," said Barela, half saluting. "Anything you say, Boss."

The two Mexicans remained near the closed door. Gorda wore the Apache red band around his head and long leggings and a red flannel shirt. Tomas showed jagged teeth beneath a conical sombrero and was draped in a serape. They wore two revolvers, long Bowies and carried rifles. The New York men stared at them with hostility, these were strange people whose very presence brought discomfort.

Only Tanner spoke Spanish. "You bring a message?"

"Si. The Commandant Santa Ferra wishes to make the exchange tonight, at the encampment of the herd," Tomas said.

Tanner translated. Maxton demanded, "Now, why the hell does he want that? He's got to bring in the herd tomorrow. What is this?"

Tanner asked the question, listened, then started, turning to Maxton, exclaiming, "Logan. They know Logan's here. They say he's poison, they want the money before they come in. Then they'll take care of

Logan. El Puma wants Logan."

Johnson said, "There, you see? Logan! Is he a copper?"

Tanner inquired, then said to Maxton, "All they know is that he's dangerous, he killed some of them in Mexico, he's got some connection with Colonel Barty."

"Barty!"

Tomas grinned and said, "Si, si. The Commandant said you should know this."

"Barty!" Maxton sat up straight. "Okay. Tell them we'll be there after dark."

Tanner conveyed the message. The two Mexicans, Indian and halfbreed, bowed and went as quickly and silently as they had come.

Maxton said, "Barty, the double-crossing bastard! Playin' both sides of the fence. Buyin' up the Cross B and the Rockin' Chair. Logan's nothin' but his agent. That smooth talkin', fat little bastard."

"We goin' to take money out to El Puma?" asked Johnson uneasily. "They bad people."

"They happen to be our bad people," Maxton said. "They can't do nothin' to us until they sell the cattle to Carraway. Get it? And then they may get Logan, save us the trouble. Sure, we're goin' to take them the money for the stuff from their wagons. You bet we are!"

"Reckon he didn't want to bring in the wagons," Sunny ruminated. "Just the beef. Reckon he's goin' to hold the loot and put the responsibility on us."

"We can handle it," Maxton said. "Between him and us what chance has Logan got?"

They thought about that, satisfied.

The day was waning. Logan mixed eggs in a large bowl while Barty and Ambrose watched. "You'd starve without me," he told them. "I'll need more wood. Stir yourself, one of you."

Ambrose sauntered out of the house. Logan looked hard at Barty and asked, "What about the dam up on the creek above Carraway's boundary line and mine?"

"It'll help the whole countryside," Barty said evasively. "What objection you all got?"

"Custom of the country. It's my water," Logan told him. "War in the country doesn't help anything."

"What makes you think I got anything to do with it?" Barty caressed his whiskers, his eyes blank.

"Carraway, I have learned, is neither that smart nor that tough. In the courthouse I examined deeds, all kinds of deeds. Your name appears on some marginal land."

Barty said, "You're smart."

"Too smart?" Logan sliced thick pieces from a ham. "Is that what you're trying to tell me?"

"I sent you here to do a job. . . ."

"And to pay off my mortgage and to buy some cattle." He did not reveal that he had paid up Badger's mortgage and therefore had no money to buy cattle. "Did you think El Puma would do business with me in preference to Carraway? And Simon Maxton?"

Barty said, "I got a stake here. I told you that in the beginning."

"Your land's worth nothing except nuisance value," Logan said, putting platters on the stove shelf to warm them. Ambrose came in with the wood and he exercised the pot lifter, replenishing the fire, taking down a big frypan of iron and arranging the ham slices in it. "Why don't you level with me, Barty?"

Barty said in his shorthand manner, "I am levelling. Seems to me you ain't got a thing on Maxton yet. Annie Morgan got killed behind your back."

"You didn't tell me she was working for you. I didn't know she was stealing from you and Maxton," Logan pointed out.

"She wasn't exactly workin' for me." Barty actually squirmed. "I was usin' her to get a line on Maxton."

"I see." He was beginning to see, he thought. His collar seemed very tight about his neck. His head, he thought, was probably right in that noose which Barty had fashioned. If Barty learned that he was even remotely aware of this, he could be dead in a very short time. He dissembled. "That's clever, all right. Now, what you want from me is evidence to convict Maxton of dealing in drugs."

"That's what I hired you for."

"I can get it tonight."

"That's what Washington wants."

"And you want Maxton destroyed for your purposes."

"Carraway can be managed. Badger's a drunk. You . . . I figure we're partners up here."

Oh, sure, thought Logan. Partners. Barty never had a partner in his life. I'm expendable, that's what I am. Nobody gets a free ride from Barty. It all comes out neat as a Chinese box puzzle when you look at it from afar. Neat — and lethal. He wondered where Ambrose, the simple, lackadaisical former Texas Ranger came in. The short end, also?

Aloud he said, "I like that. You're telling me that if I fix it for Maxton, we've got a deal in land and cattle. Right?"

"Right." Barty unhooded his eyes and smiled beneath the mustache, looking like a benevolent, small brown bear.

"Come and get it," Logan said, stirring the eggs into another, smaller pan. "I mean you, Ambrose. I put it together, you can watch it, take it off and serve it."

"Sure," said Ambrose amiably, lounging to the stove.

Barty asked, "Ain't you goin' to eat?"

"It's getting dark," said Logan. He sliced a piece of bread, buttered it, thrust a hunk of ham in its middle. "This'll do me as I ride along."

"Ambrose'll be in later."

"No," said Logan. "Maxton knows Ambrose, right? Therefore, keep him here until early morning at earliest. I take it you won't be in when El Puma brings the herd to Bailey?"

"Wouldn't do," said Barty defensively. "Can't be seen. This is your mission. You can report to me here."

"You can milk the cow in the morning," Logan told him. "Plenty of bread and bacon and eggs."

"I'll make do," Barty told him with dignity.

"I ain't purely helpless."

Logan looked at Ambrose. "You all right, amigo?"

Ambrose was gingerly stirring the eggs. "I'm all right. See you tomorrow."

Logan lifted a hand to Barty and went out and saddled the black horse. His mind was whirling so that his head ached. He chewed on the sandwich for a moment. He knew what he should do, there was no question about it.

He should ride straight north, out of the county, to Denver, then to San Francisco. He should borrow some money, gamble for a stake, then take a ship to some distant place where neither Barty nor the United States Government could find him.

Barty was terrific, he ruminated. If it had not been for the link with Annie Morgan it might have been impossible for Logan to guess the rest. Annie and the fact that Barty's derringer had been up his sleeve since they had met at Cross B and Ambrose had never, for one instant until he went out for the kindling, been any place but behind him. Logan never missed this bit of opera, that was his business.

The little brown man was too smart behind those whiskers. He figured far ahead of such as Maxton and El Puma. He counted on people acting according to their nature.

Logan was sucker enough to go along, he realized, riding up the hill toward the cave where Annie Morgan lay. Further, he was going to try a cross of his own. He was going to make people act *against* their nature. The game would be decided on this basis, either Barty was smarter than he, or he was smarter than Barty. It was as simple as that.

Packing the blanketed body on the black horse was a problem but he had managed this before. He rode down the short distance to the Lazy Dog ranch house. It was fully dark by then and the lamps were lit in the main building. He hallooed from the yard, dismounting. As he expected, Paul Crown appeared, rifle in hands.

"Hi, Paul. Mind giving me a hand here?" Logan said conversationally.

Crown came close, sniffed, retreated. "That there smells like a corpse!"

From the house Mel Carraway called, "What's goin' on there?"

"Bring a lantern, Mel," suggested Logan. "Want to show you something. Keep Susan in the house."

"You get the hell outa here," Carraway howled. "Nobody around here wants to see you."

Logan said, "I'm aware of that. But I want you to see what I have here."

He managed the body singlehanded. The light from the doorway threw an oblong in which he lay Annie Morgan, untying the blanket with swift hands, throwing it aside.

Paul Crown said, "Good God in his heaven!" not profanely, staring.

Carraway demanded, "What is it, Paul?"

Susan appeared behind Carraway. Paul Crown said, "You don't need no lantern. But stay inside, Miss Susan, stay away from this."

Carraway had to come forward. He moved slowly, his Colt in his hand, suspicious. He saw the bruised features of Annie Morgan and sucked in his breath. He stood stock still. Susan poised uncertainly in the doorway, he motioned to her to remain there.

Logan said, "Thought you'd want to see some of your partner's work."

"Maxton?" asked Crown.

"And his little bunch. They killed her, finally. With that dope they're running through Bailey. The drugs Mel doesn't want to know about."

"She was in on it?"

"In part. The story's too long to tell right now. I'm just going to lay out some things I believe. You people can take it from there."

He drew a breath and then went on, "El Puma brings in the drugs from Mexico, probably in his wagons. Thousand and thousands of dollars worth. Maxton ships it to all parts of the country at a big profit. Then you buy the wetbacks which let El Puma travel without anyone thinking of drug traffic. Meantime Maxton distributes enough heroin and morphine in Bailey to keep a bunch of addicts ready to fight for more. Men you don't even notice, cheap gunmen and tinhorns who will turn into killers if they are deprived."

Crown said slowly, "Highpockets. Sloppy Joe. It bothered me, the way they been. Simple-like. Loco."

"You've noticed," said Logan. "Rose Maguire was hooked. Doc Sutton's been trying to taper her off it. You see the way it is, Mel? You see how Bailey is? You see what can happen if Maxton keeps growing in importance?"

"He was talkin' about the legislature, in Santa Fe," said Carraway wonderingly. "Once he said he might be governor some day."

"Yes," said Logan. "It's happened. The biggest crook getting the biggest job. Not enough law to show the people who they really are, these crooks."

"Are you some kind of law?" demanded Carraway. "Is that why you're here?"

"Part of it. Tomorrow El Puma comes in. He'll be expecting you to buy the herd."

"I got to think." Mel turned instinctively toward the house where Susan waited. "You better come in."

Crown asked, "What do I do with Annie?"

"Put her in the barn," suggested Logan. "Wrap her good and tight. We may need her body tomorrow."

"For what?"

"If Mel decides my way, you could come to the funeral. You know — Ford and the other one Barela killed. You could bring her for planting."

Crown said, "If Mel says so."

Logan went into the house. The room was huge, with a beamed ceiling and a fireplace that would accommodate an eight-foot log. There were Navajo rugs on the planked floor, worn but colorful and comfortable, as was the rawhide furniture. Yet there were frilled curtains at the window and doilies where they were neither attractive nor needed. Susan was glowing, beautiful in the light of the high lamps, but her lips were set in a straight line, her chin was slightly out-thrust.

She said, "I heard."

"Well?" asked Logan. Carraway stood with his back to the fireplace, swaying back and forth, new lines in his round, immature face.

"I say we stay out of it. I say we stay here and defend what we have. What you have left to us."

Logan shrugged. "That's up to you and Mel. Just one thought, if you stay out of it and Maxton wins, what happens?"

"We do business with Maxton. We may not approve of him, but we can get along with him."

Caraway started to speak, caught a look from Susan, refrained. Logan walked toward the door.

"There's Mama Rugelo and her son. And Magin and Doc Sutton and a lot of people we knew in the old days, when the world was simpler. Nothing people. And Rose Maguire, who went to school with us."

"And became a slut!"

"But is alive and trying to recover from the drug habit. No use to moralize with you, Susan, I can see that. But if those people are destroyed, where's your town? What good the valley and the ranches?"

"We remain apart," she said coldly. "We still have Lazy Dog and a seed herd. We'll make out."

"Until Maxton decides to take over." He

wheeled upon Carraway. "Like the dam they're building up yonder, eh, Mel? Got you puzzled, hasn't it?"

Carraway said, "We'll take care of the water."

Logan deliberately scoffed at him. "You don't even know who's building the dam. I'll tell you this much, it's not Maxton. What does Maxton know about dams? You never were quite bright, Mel. Don't try and figure it out, that's not your dish. Try and think of the valley and of the way our fathers settled here and of the people who worked for us and who came to Bailey when it was a crossroads. Balance all that against money in Maxton's bank. Maxton's bank!"

He managed to laugh as he went out to the black horse. He did not feel like laughing. He had seen the greed and selfishness in Susan. He knew she dominated Mel. He had not enlisted allies, as he had hoped.

Paul Crown came into the light and said, "Pasquale, he couldn't find out who was buildin' the dam. He's got more sense than Mel any old day."

"You listen at windows."

"Around here you better had," Crown said. "Hate to put down a lady, but I like to know when I'm bein' undercut. She don't like me none."

"I'll need help in town tomorrow."

"I hired to Mel," Crown said simply. "You know, I kinda like the dumb slob."

"You object to a woman ruling a man," Logan said. "I'll say it again. I'll need every gun tomorrow. Ed Badger ran out on me. Got him doped up to keep him out of trouble. There's nobody but Sutton and Magin, both scared, and maybe some people, Spanish-Americans."

"And you."

"Too many of them. Far too many."

"You'll do for a heap," Crown said. "But I'm hired to Carraway. It's kind of all I've got, y' see? I lose that and where am I?"

Logan said, "I'll be looking for you."

He rode toward Bailey. The night was fitful, the moon had vanished. Thunderheads gathered over the Kneeling Nun and Mob Hill was hidden from his view. He increased the pace, his thoughts sour.

Susan Badger, he thought, what a change. Or had she always been selfish beyond his knowledge? Had he been a callow fool not to recognize her egotism? Had the gentleness of her acquiescence that time long ago been merely a lure to entrap him? How could he know?

Women, he thought, were ever fickle, ever treacherous. He had pursued the right course, using them and tossing them to the wolves. He had stayed alive and free by this process. He was lucky, he thought, his spirits rising, spurring the black horse ahead of the impending storm.

He could still quit this rangdoodle, he reminded himself. He could make a play tonight, take a chance on confusing everyone and get on the stage — or ride out — with Dora Bell and her grubstake. They could open a gambling house together, as she had suggested. He knew of places where he would be welcome. Luke Short was operating the White Elephant in Fort Worth, Luke had settled down.

The first drops of rain lit upon his face and he came alive to the present. He gave the black horse a blow while he donned the poncho from the roll behind his saddle. He was on the road between the hills and now the storm was coming apace. He knew these storms; they were lethal to the unsuspecting rider.

He spurred the black. There was one low spot ahead which he must pass before the river formed and came down from the mountain. Flash floods were the most dangerous hazard to travelers in these parts, he was well aware. Thunder rolled and darkness fell complete. He found his exact position by the first flash of zigzag lightning and knew it was up to the black horse whether he would make it or not.

There was the other choice, still. He could turn and ride back to Rocking Chair. Or to Cross B, facing down Barty, taking his chances on bluffing the two Texans. Or he could head across country to Silver by the long route, seeking shelter from the rain, escaping in the morning. There were plenty of alternatives. For one moment he was deeply tempted.

Then he thought of the girl in the hayloft. The others, the Suttons and Magins, even the Rugelos, had allowed Maxton to move in and take over. They could sink or swim so far as he was concerned, Logan thought. But to the girl he was indebted. It was not that she was attractive. He had just been given a lesson in the way it could be with a female he had once thought was the most attractive in the world.

The hell with it, he then thought. My life is my own, I can do what I want with it. If death wants me let him come now or let him come tomorrow. I ride with him.

He was not going to make the gulley which formed a dip in the trail, he knew at once. It was up to the horse. He was in truth riding with death. He laughed into the storm, welcoming it as that which had freed him from making a wrong decision.

They hit the flash flood full tilt, the only way to attempt it. The water was over his head. The black breasted it and began swimming with celerity and grace. It was slow, but when they were in peril of being swept away, Logan knew to gently change direction. The distance was not great to higher land, but the current was twice that of a raging river. He slipped from the saddle, fearing to tire the black. He held onto its tail, using one arm to help in the battle.

They went under twice. The horse faltered and Logan fought his way to its head. They breasted the fury side by side as he tried to offer encouragement, his mouth filling with water, clinging to the bridle, fighting, fighting for every inch.

After an eternity horsehoe changed upon stone. Logan swam with all his strength. The black stumbled, almost fell, regained footing. Then the two of them were on the other side of the torrent, gasping for breath, the man clinging to the animal.

When he could speak, Logan addressed the horse, "You never know with Mister Death. He might be saving us for tomorrow, you think of that? He may have been laughing at us, the way we struggled to get to where he waits for us. But we're here. You see? It means we have to go on. One escape, I have learned, is nothing. Mister Death is a clever one . . . and he knows he can't lose! Sooner or later . . . if sooner, well, then let it be."

It was still raining steadily when they came to Bailey. Every light seemed to be on, shining starkly through the night. Maxton's places were roaring, the addicts were enjoying free dream dust, thought Logan, readying themselves for whatever Maxton demanded on the morrow — or this dour night. He rode inside the livery stable, soaking wet.

There was a lantern shining in the end stall and Monterey came quickly to care for the black. Logan shook raindrops from hat and poncho as the girl also came from the stall.

He looked at the girl. "Will you take a chance with me?"

"Mr. Logan! This is so sudden," she simpered.

He said grimly, "It may be sudden death."

"I can't stay here much longer," she rejoined blithely. "My pants are itchin' me. What did you have in mind, Mr. Logan, sir?"

"Get over to the hotel by the back lots in

about fifteen minutes. We're going to break into Maxton's upstairs rooms. You know the layout."

Logan felt free and light footed, walking to the hotel. There was something about the New York gamin. She kept him always amused, at least. He saw Pedro lurking in the depths of the lobby, noted a rifle handy against the wall, spoke reassuringly to the boy, went upstairs to his room. He undressed and rubbed himself pink with a rough towel. Then he put on dry underwear and pants and a clean shirt and saw to his weapons, drying them, reloading them with fresh ammunition. There was a tap on the door and he admitted Dora Bell.

She was drenched. She looked like a boy in her tight riding pants — but then he looked at her shirtwaist and she looked like a grown woman. He said contritely, "I should have given you my poncho."

She removed a scarf from her dank locks and said crossly, "I hope you've got a comb and brush and some kind of decent hat for me. I can borrow one of your shirts."

She took off her wet upper covering. He plucked a shirt from his bag and tossed it to her. Unconcernedly, she was using his towel to dry herself. She grabbed his brush and vigorously attacked her hair, leaving the shirt on the chair next to the mirror.

He said, "That dark one will do it. We're breaking and entering tonight. Tippy-toe, if you please." He tried to be neither too curious nor too abashed at her partially undressed state. He felt he had to match her nonchalance.

She said, "I sure look like . . . mustn't say hell. We going to burglarize Maxton's?"

"For a package of drugs," he said. "Annie Morgan brought it in. They should have packed it for shipping on tomorrow's stage with the rest of it . . . El Puma's delivery. They must be picking up from El Puma right now."

She said, "They been gone some time. Suppose they come back while we're moochin' around up there?"

"I'll loan you my little gun." He watched her closely for her reaction.

She reached into the front of her trousers and produced the nickel plated .32. "Better see if it'll work. You wouldn't have bullets for it, I reckon."

"You reckon right." He dried the little weapon.

" 'Reckon,' " she repeated. "That's western lingo. I'm a larnin'."

He moved to put the gun on the wash stand and his hand brushed her bare arm.

They stared at one another in the mirror for a moment. Her mouth pinched in, her lips grew full in the next instant, her eyes widened and she leaned toward him. He held his breath.

Then she gave him the pixie grin and moved away. "Business as usual? To be continued in our next, like in the Ned Buntline novels?"

"Not like in the Buntline novels," he said.

"All right." She donned the dark shirt.

He found a black vest and gave it to her. It was snug when she buttoned it. He said, "You're some kind of a somethin'. That's western talk."

"I like it," she said gravely. "Tell me what we're gonna do, now."

"Get in the back way. Then you lead me."

"It'll be in their office," she decided. "You'll tell me when to use the gun?"

"I'll tell you. Hold low, aim for the belt."

"Dirty pool," she commented. "But it'll get 'em, I can figure that. Should we dance?"

"You're in a big hurry all of a sudden."

She said, "Logan, what they done to Annie ain't a patch on what Maxton would do to me. You understand?"

He had a sudden revolting picture of what was meant by the plain-spoken girl. "It won't happen."

"Not while I got a shot left. Thing is, when I get scared this bad, I want to get it over with."

They went out the rear entrance across the littered yards to which he was becoming accustomed. She was so quickly acquiescent he remembered her face in the mirror, tight, pale and for a sickening instant he wondered — had she been planted from the start? Was she Maxton's spy? Was her succeeding expression contrition? Was she leading him into a trap?

It was too late to do anything about it now. He watched the street, chose a moment when three reeling drunks or drug users were making a scene, led her swiftly across and to the rear of the Palace.

He whispered, "You know the way. Go ahead."

She immediately ran up the stairs on light feet and he felt a twinge of guilt for suspecting her. He had to hurry to keep up with her. They got into the hallway and stood listening, hearts pounding. There was the sound of high revelry from the saloon below.

She mouthed silently, "My room." She went in before he could stop her. Now he was wary as a deer in an open field, gun drawn, flat against the wall. Then she came out and she was wearing dry riding pants and giggling. "No itch, now, let's go," she said.

The door to the office was locked, but Logan exercised a limber bit of steel to open it. "Stay on the right side of the door, so you'll be ready if it opens. Be ready."

"Get crackin'," she said. "I'm scared pea green."

He saw the closet in the corner and made straight for it. There was no need for elaborate concealment, he thought. Maxton had everything under control. The package was in plain sight. It was not very large. It was addressed to "Maxton Forwarding Co. Ltd., Kansas City, Mo."

He picked it up and she breathed, "Sunny. On his way."

The room was in darkness except for reflected light. He put the package under his arm and ran to her. They stood tight together to the right of the doorway. The latch rattled. Sunny was trying it. After a moment they began to breathe easily — and together. She was very warm and soft.

Then the knob of the door slowly turned. The key clicked. Sunny was about to make a small raid of his own, Logan thought, putting Dora behind him.

In that moment he knew he would learn

about her. She had the revolver. Sunny was coming in front of him, she had only to pull the trigger and Logan would be on his journey with Mister Death.

The door opened slowly. Sunny stepped into the room. Logan swung the muzzle of his Colt.

Sunny went down on his knees, facing away from the two intruders. Logan hit him again, very hard, at the base of the skull.

Then he reached for Dora, grabbed her hand and rushed her down the hall to the back stairs. They were in the rain and across the street to Magin's place within the minute. Before they went inside he put his arm around her shoulders. She slumped against him and to his astonishment she was weeping.

"It's all right. It's over. We've got what we wanted."

She sniffled. "For a minute there, you didn't trust me. You thought I'd fink on you."

He said, "That's not true!"

"You let me go ahead. Don't tell me. You didn't believe."

He lied, "Dora, I'm a careful man. But as to trusting you — with my life, any time."

She said, "Sure . . . now. Don't try to fool me, Logan. I been around. I seen the elephant." She shook her head. "It's okay. What else? What could I expect? It's okay, Logan. Come on, I'm gettin' all wet again."

He felt lower than a snake's belly, opening the door and watching her go into Magin's back room. The corpses were in their coffins in a corner and she shuddered. Magin came, scared, eyebrows raised.

Logan extended the package. "Put it under Ford's head for a pillow."

"All that is heroin?" Magin's cupidity was plain.

"I wouldn't know," said Logan coldly. "If I don't get it back after tomorrow's rangdoodle, however, there'll be a dead wood whittler around here."

"All right, all right. But it's worth a fortune. Thousands." Magin took it reverently and went to the casket of the dead tinhorn.

Logan hastily led Dora into the hospital room. Ed Badger was still sleeping. Doc Sutton sat beside Rose's cot, holding her hand. They stared at Dora and Logan.

"We've got Maxton nailed. If we survive," Logan told them. "El Puma's coming in and Maxton's onto me by now; he has to be. I'll be scarce tonight. You'll have to tough it out. Have you arms?"

"Shotguns," said Sutton. "I don't think

he'll have time to bother with us, do you? He doesn't think we're important. He can handle us any time."

"It's your best chance," said Logan. "The big fight will be tomorrow morning."

"Who will begin it?"

Logan told him grimly, "I will, before they do. I'll be talking to some other people, Mama Rugelo and such folk. Good luck to you all."

He took Dora out into the rain again, and they got back to the livery stable without incident. Monterey was resigned by now to their presence. They climbed up into the loft. Logan realized he was dead tired. It had been a long, hard day. He stretched, removed his boots. Alongside him, Dora did the same. Monterey found two horse blankets which were dry.

Dora said, "You take one and go in that corner, where you can see the yard."

Logan blinked surprise at her command.

In another moment she had spread the blanket over them and was snuggling close to Logan. He put his arms around her and she sighed.

"I don't care," she said in his ear. "Even if you didn't trust me. When it hits me, I just go over the bridge and into the drink. Kiss me, Logan."

He kissed her. It was the least he could do after his lack of trust in her.

Chapter Eleven

The sun was high, the storm had blown over the mountains. On Boot Hill the silent German duo were digging a third grave. Tanner and Mose Johnson scowled, asked questions, were greeted by blank stares, turned and went rapidly to the livery stable.

Monterey was puttering about the yard. He said, "I know nothing, senors. Nothing."

They examined Logan's black horse, found him dry and rested, munching hay, conveying nothing to their suspicions. They went back up the street where Mama Rugelo's place seemed to contain the only waking citizens at breakfast. They slammed into Magin's place.

Rose and Ed Badger slept, oblivious. Dr. Sutton put a finger to his lips, ordered them from the hospital with an imperious gesture. They went into the room where the corpses lay — and stared at the composed features of the dead Annie Morgan. They grabbed Magin and shoved him hard against the wall.

He moaned, "Ain't you got no respect for the dead?"

"Annie Morgan. Where'd she come from?"

"A wagon. Early this morning," he said truthfully. "Dumped her off."

"You're lyin'."

"Look . . . this here note."

It was a piece of lined paper that read, "We found her. You plant her . . . Friends of Annie."

"Whyn't you tell Simon?"

"You all wasn't there," whined Magin. "Sunny wasn't in the bar."

Tanner said to Johnson, "That's right. We better get to Simon quick."

They departed, leaving Magin to slide to the floor. He was wearing his funeral costume of tailcoat and tall hat and he was scared to his boots.

Logan came from behind a stack of caskets, holstering his revolver. "Paul Crown brought her in."

"It was him, all right. I'm scared, Dan'l."

"You've been scared all your life. Now you can bury these people and stay out of what'll happen today. If you're lucky, you might even get your town back again."

Magin got slowly to his feet. He went to the wall where the coffins were placed, selected a lid, came to put it over the body of Ford, the tinhorn. "All that money in there," he complained.

"I'll want those packages," Logan warned. "They'd better be there."

"I ain't got the nerve to swipe 'em," Magin told him.

Logan went into the hospital room. Ed Badger opened one eye, grunted, swung his legs down over the edge of the cot. Rose and Dr. Sutton now sat side by side on her bed, shotguns at hand.

"Stay on Boot Hill with those guns," Logan said. "Just be ready if we lose on the streets."

"It'll be the biggest funeral Bailey ever saw," said Rose.

"You're lucky not to be a fourth," Logan told her.

He turned to Badger. "I suppose you want a drink?"

"What the hell did he give me?" Badger stared at Sutton. "I want water." He drank from a pitcher. "What happened yesterday after I got swacked?"

"You were going to gun me down for giving you back your ranch. Your dear little daughter would have liked that. She's mad because I beat on Mel for awhile. But when I showed him a woman beat to death by Maxton, he quieted down. Annie Morgan, that was, or do you know?"

Badger rumbled, "I'm an old man. . . ."

"In his prime, but trying to duck life by being pickled in alcohol," Logan interrupted. "And I thought you could handle Cross B and Rocking Chair for me . . . for us. Maybe I should have picked Carraway."

Badger said, "Just a cotton pickin' minute. Any day I ain't smarter than that clod, drunk or sober, I will quit."

"All right. I'll buy that. Haven't got time to argue. There's a war coming any minute. You want to ride out or do you want to stick?"

Badger fumbled beneath the cot. His black-butted guns looked dangerous even in their holsters. "If I could have maybe some coffee, a hunk of bread?"

"He needs it, for strength," said Dr. Sutton.

Logan's eyes gleamed, watching the practiced, startlingly youthful hands buckle the belt, adjust the hang of the old single-action Colt revolvers. He said, "Well, Ed. Welcome back to the valley."

"It's been a kinda long trip," Badger acknowledged. "You ride with John Barleycorn, you go far places."

"Follow me," Logan said. He took a last look at the couple holding hands, added softly, "Good luck. See you when the fun begins."

The Rugelo family was extensive. The two men went through back doors and up secluded alleys. Three women in serapes covered them as they went across the street to the livery. There was food beneath the colorful shawls. Sarge and Dora Bell were waiting. Danger seemed to make everyone very hungry.

A lanky rider turned into the livery yard. Monterey went to him but Logan called, "It's all right. Welcome to the party, Ambrose."

"Thought I oughta see what's goin' on here," drawled the tall man, dismounting

"Have a taco," said Logan. "And set awhile. You'll find out what's going on."

Ambrose shook hands with Ed Badger and said, "Owe you for some fodder, man and beast. Logan said you wouldn't mind."

"Forget it," Badger told him. "Any friend of Daniel's, any time."

"Thanks," said Ambrose. He did not smile as he accepted food and repaired to the stable, out of view of passersby.

Maxton walked the floor of the office. Sunny sat with his bandaged head in his hands, occasionally moaning. Tanner repeatedly examined his weapons, deadly serious. Mose Johnson crouched at the table like a black leopard.

Maxton said, "Logan. I should've known from the start. He got Buffalo. He took the twist away. He brought Annie back. And he slugged Sunny and stole the stuff."

"He's got a crooked mind," Sunny said. "He acts like some big crook."

"Colonel Barty sent him," Maxton said. "That damn Barty is onto something."

"Barty smart," mooned Johnson. "Just lemme get my dukes on Logan, thassall."

"His horse is here. Why don't we go out and find him and take care of him?" Tanner asked.

"It's his home town. You don't go huntin' a smart gun in his own place," Maxton said. "The herd's comin' in. We got to let the cattle through town for Carraway. Then we'll see."

"They're buryin' Ford and them this mornin'. We goin' to the funeral?"

Maxton went to the closet, opened it, kicked at four large packages. "That El Puma. He was grinnin' like an ape last night. Supposin' he took it in his head to get smart like Logan?"

"We got too many people," Tanner said. "We'll be watchin' that bunch of his'n."

"Sunny, you stay here," Maxton decided. "Tanner, you and me, we go to the funeral. It's on top of the hill and we can keep our eyes open. Johnson, you nose around and look for the missin' stuff and Logan and whatever. Take Highpockets and a couple others along. And tell everybody again not to let the stage leave without I check it. We got men blockin' every road, haven't we?"

"Sure," said Sunny. "But Logan don't need to use roads. He don't need to take the black horse. He could be gone from here with the dame long since, right after he slugged me. If it was him who did it."

"Who else?" demanded Maxton.

"El Puma?"

Maxton slammed the door of the closet, locked it, put the key in his pocket. "We got maybe fifty people. If we can't handle the damn British-Mexican and find Logan and clean house, there's somethin' wrong."

"This town needs a lesson," Tanner said. "We been too easy on them Mexes. They gotta be hidin' Logan."

"I ketch him, I take him to pieces," Johnson promised.

"And watch that El Puma," ordered Maxton. "It's got so you can't trust nobody no more."

Crown went into the bunkhouse, where Mel Carraway had been sleeping since the advent of Susan Badger. He sat down on his own bed and took out a jackknife and began worrying at a limber leather strap. There had been loud voices late in the night from the big house and Mel had obviously just arisen.

"Everything ready for the new herd?" asked Mel.

"Pasquale says so. He's got a couple men to help."

Mel went to the wash basin and poured water. He snorted through brief ablutions, ran a comb through his thinning, fair hair and turned to Crown.

"You aint' talkin'."

"Nope."

"You think I'm wrong not to side Logan."

"Yep."

"Why don't you go on in town, then?"

"You firin' me, Mel?"

"No, I got no cause to fire you."

Crown said, "And I ain't gonna give you none. You been fair with me. You lemme take Annie's body in."

"You been a good man for me," said Mel. "Damn!"

Crown was silent, slicing the strap with great delicacy.

Carraway said, "You think she's runnin' me."

No reply.

Carraway said, "Well, you're right. She's runnin' me. Why's she got to have Cross B and Rockin' Chair? There's plenty here on my place. This here's a good spread."

"Unless the dam cuts off the water," suggested Crown. "It could cut it off from any of the three ranches."

"I'll find out who's dammin' the stream. I can deal for water, Dan ain't that kind, to block me out."

"Good man, that Logan," said Crown.

Carraway swallowed and then said, "Susan don't think so. Says he's footloose. Thinks he'll cut me because of her."

"You think so?"

"Damn it, no. He never was like that."

Crown said, "Well, it's betwixt you and her. Not for me to say."

"Her old man. . . ." He thought a moment. "You think Ed will come to life for Logan?"

"Logan's got his ways. Could be."

Mel said heavily, "I argued all night and by damn, here I go again."

Crown looked up at him. "That's why I ain't quittin', Mel. You slow sometimes, but nobody can say you ain't one to see things through."

The big man slammed out of the bunkhouse. Crown finished trimming his strap, began to whistle. Then he took out his Colt, reached for his pack and began to oil and clean the spotless weapon.

The roof slanted toward the rear of the stable. Logan lay flat, looking through his field glasses. Alongside him Dora Bell admired the countryside.

"Never get days like this in New York," she said. "You can see a mile in each direction."

Logan said, "Just about. Here, take a look northward, on top of that hill. You see anything?"

After a moment she said, "Looks like a man with another pair of glasses. The sun hits off 'em."

He took back the binoculars. "Man with a beard? A slight resemblance to General Grant?"

"Yep," she said. "Beard and all."

He scanned the horizon to the south. The cloud of dust he had been gauging was coming closer, he could almost distinguish the cattle. Time was growing short.

Across the street a hand waved. Pedro Rugelo and some others were on the roof of the hotel. Logan motioned them to keep down behind the parapet, out of sight.

There was the sound of a wagon in the street. Magin came out of his place, followed by the two big Germans carrying a coffin. Dr. Sutton was driving the flat bodied farm wagon which served for a hearse in this instance. Logan watched while the other two caskets were put into place.

Maxton and Tanner came from the Palace and waited, several of their people behind them, gamblers, tinhorns, all armed as usual. Mose Johnson and Highpockets, a weird looking, long-legged tough, and a couple of others had been going up and down and in and out for the past hour. Everyone was spotted, Logan thought. He gave Magin a signal to hasten the procession to Boot Hill where the three graves yawned.

Logan said, "I'll say it once more. You can get out of this."

She kissed him on the cheek. "And miss all the fun?"

"It will not be fun." He had never felt low in spirits before a fight until now. "Good people may die, down there in the street, up on Boot Hill. That man who looks like General Grant knows it. That's why he's yonder. Make sure you stay right here."

"I like it when you talk western," she said, smiling her gamin's smile. " 'You heah?' " she mimicked. "I like it when you forget all that school stuff."

He said, "The funeral procession is starting. I have to go down. Will you stay here, now?"

She waved at him. "Just take care of yourself. I'll be coverin' you."

He lowered himself through the transom trap and descended a ladder into the hayloft. The horse blankets still lay disarranged as they had left them.

Ambrose and Ed Badger were in the rear stall. Logan joined them, with Monterey standing guard, shotgun close at hand but not visible from the street.

Logan said, "Magin will be here in a minute. Ed, you can join the funeral without arousing suspicion. The wetbacks are just at the edge of town by now. There'll be confusion when they come through."

Badger said, "I'll follow Maxton up Boot Hill."

"Right," said Logan. "Ambrose, they know you. Better stick with me until the ball opens."

"Yeah," said Ambrose.

"You all right?" Logan asked Badger. "You savvy the layout?"

"Ha!" said the older man. "It'll be some funeral."

The creak of Magin's wagon became louder. Ed Badger hitched at his two guns and went out of the stable. Maxton and the others scarcely gave him a glance as he fell into line with Perdita Rugelo and her daughter. The procession was meager and straggling. Rose Maguire had joined it since Logan had last looked and this he did not like.

"Rose is half-sick," he muttered. "She shouldn't make Doc nervous this way."

Ambrose said, "Be a lot of nervish ones in a bit."

"I hate to open this," Logan fretted. "There'll be too many people hurt."

"You got the evidence to arrest Maxton." Ambrose was lugubrious.

"You know better than that. I don't carry a badge."

"Yeah," said Ambrose. "That's right."

The wagon bearing the caskets began climbing Boot Hill. Logan called up to the rooftop, "Where are the cattle now?"

Dora Bell's bright voice said, "Comin' on. There's a heap of riders along, Logan. They got rifles in their hands, all of 'em."

"All this about the Colonel's property around Bailey. It's not that important. Even the dam — that can only lead to a range war or court litigation. There's something wrong with this entire setup," Logan ruminated aloud. "You sure you don't know something that would clear it up?"

"Who, me? I'm just along," said Ambrose. "I shoot pretty good, once I haul out the gun. Colonel said to back you up."

"Uh-huh," Logan said. "I see." He went to the wide door of the stable. "The watering trough, I think. You got any ideas?"

Ambrose said, "The hitchin' rack. Good thick posts. Just gimme a holler."

The street seemed empty as Logan ran to the zinc-lined trough and knelt behind it. Then he saw fat Santos Barela standing guard at the bank, gawking toward El Puma's advancing column of men and longhorn cattle. As the avalanche of beef and horsemen gained speed, Barela's face registered surprise, nothing more.

For a moment Logan was tempted to shout, to warn the witless Marshal. Then he thought of the clumsy, ruthless killing of Frenchy and turned to look at Boot Hill.

Dinty Magin, in the absence of the circuit riding preacher, had his prayerbook in his hand. The crowd was loosely gathered around the three graves. The two big Germans were putting the coffins in place. Maxton and Tanner and the others of that gang were bunched, off to one side.

Ambrose said, "What's that Mex up to?" his voice rising in real alarm.

The cattle were thundering, far too fast for a peaceful amble through town. The horns clanked together in the narrow thoroughfare, adding to their frenzy. They were wild-eyed, running on long legs. Vaqueros wielded cruel whips on the flanks of any possible strays.

Logan caught a glimpse of El Puma in his dandified garments, pulling up a roan horse at the bank. There was a single shot.

Santos Barela fell sideways and rolled. Two big riders smashed at the door of the bank.

"It's a raid," Ambrose said, and swore to himself, glancing unconsciously and instinctively toward the far hilltop where Colonel Barty was watching.

"You're surprised?" Logan fired once with the rifle but missed as El Puma followed his men into the bank. "I thought the Colonel knew everything."

Atop the hill where the serried graves lay in rows Maxton heard the shots. He came around, and all his men with him. They stared, then began running down the slope. Two hard-riding vaqueros immediately began to mill the leaders of the herd, cutting off Maxton and his men from the town.

Logan stood up and waved his hat. Young Pedro, on the roof of the hotel, understood.

At the bank, two of El Puma's men had spotted Mose Johnson and Highpockets coming from behind the restaurant and were firing at them.

Highpockets went down as if cut in two, but Johnson ducked and rolled, escaping the first volley. Now it was apparent that El Puma had indeed brought an army, as horsemen spurred up from the rear of the herd.

Pedro and four other riflemen fired from the hotel roof. Two of the invaders went down, screaming.

Logan yelled, "The bank!"

Pedro's people began firing at the door of the bank, splintering it with lead. The vaqueros sought cover. Tomas, The Spider, brandished a knife and raced to the hotel entrance. Logan sighted along the barrel of the rifle and squeezed off. Tomas clutched at his chest and splattered himself on the verandah.

Ambrose said, "This here is loco."

"Oh, no," Logan told him. "This here is real smart. El Puma wants all the loot."

Maxton and Tanner and the others were now trying to make their way along the street. It was a fine mixup, thought Logan, the only trouble being that he was squarely in the middle. Anyone of them would be glad to cut him down.

Logan looked at Ambrose. "Care about using the back way?"

Down the street the El Puma men were exchanging fire with those who had followed Mose Johnson on his search for the missing packages of drugs. The Mexicans were winning against the town dregs.

Ambrose said, "After you," and both ran for the rear door of the stable. As Logan skidded around the corner of the building he ran smack into Mose Johnson, who was sneaking his way, alone, to join Maxton.

The Negro snarled, "Gotcha now," and swung a powerful arm. In the fist was a sharp blade.

Before Ambrose could shoot, Logan ducked under the knife and to one side. His gun spat once. Johnson slithered away from him, fell down and lay still, a hole in his head bleeding.

"Too bad, I'd have liked to fight him," said Logan. "He was past his prime but still a professional."

Ambrose said, "I'd rather run."

It was time to move. They went down the length of Bailey over back lots. When they had come around Maxton's Palace, Logan looked worriedly toward the roof of the hotel, where the invaders had been concentrating their fire in self-defense. He saw Pedro rise up, fire, then drop back down. With relief, he went into the saloon, Ambrose at his heels.

Sunny was dead across the end of the bar, a bullet hole in his chest. Logan poured a drink from the bottle beside the dead bartender's hand and offered one to Ambrose. "Might as well let 'em fight it out. When the herd does get through town, it'll be real interesting, won't it?"

"Yeah," said Ambrose. He drank and poured another.

Logan started for the door to take a look at the action. From behind the bar arose a grisly apparition. It was Gorda, the half-breed Apache, head bloody from a wound. In his hand was a throwing knife. Logan had his back turned and was entirely unaware of danger.

Ambrose levelled his revolver and fired three times. The knife described a small arc in Logan's direction, fell to the floor. Gorda disappeared behind the bar.

Logan, crouching, spinning, shook his head. "Nice, Ambrose, nice. They die hard, don't they?"

Ambrose was reloading. "Now we're even," he said without expression. "He had you cold."

"Right," agreed Logan. He looked down the street. "Hey, this is good!"

Ambrose picked up the whiskey bottle and joined him at the door. Down the street Maxton and his bunch, including Tanner, had fought their way to the bank.

"You reckon El Puma's still in there?"

"I hope so," Logan replied. "This is a lovely war. They are killing each other off like rats."

From the bank came a rataplan of shots. Maxton ducked, but Tanner returned the fire and the other Maxton men scattered.

Logan said, "The back way seems to be ours today."

He ran into the alley and down to where he could command the rear door of the bank building. There were vaqueros strewn in awkward positions, testimony to the rigorous fire from the hotel roof.

A hail of lead almost caught him in the chest. He threw himself flat and found Ambrose beside him. They scrambled on all fours to get behind a shed.

Logan said, "El Puma's making his stand in the bank. It'll take awhile to root him out of there."

"None of our business?" suggested Ambrose.

"None at all," agreed Logan. He set sail

for the livery stable, Ambrose at his heels.

At the rear of the stable, to his dismay, was the wagon used by Magin as a hearse. A glance at Boot Hill told him they had all come down. He squirmed past the vehicle into the barn and all were present, Badger, Doc Sutton, Rose Maguire, Magin and even Dandy Blewitt.

He did not pause to remonstrate that he had told them to remain on the hill. He ran for the street to signal Pedro to reopen hostilities.

It was too late. Pedro and his friends were coming out onto the street.

Further, there was an ominous silence. Maxton and his bunch had vanished. Even as Logan ran, shouting, shooting began from the bank. Pedro staggered, ran, three of his friends fell. From the Mexican-Americans who were watching came a great, wailing cry of grief.

"I told them to stay out of it!" Logan said dully. "I tried to save lives."

Ambrose said to him, "You made a mistake, Dan'l. Never try to save 'em. It don't pay."

"El Puma and Maxton got together again. They'll be on us in a minute."

"Sure, they will," said Ambrose, looking around at the motley group. "This ain't no kind of a place. This place will burn real good."

"The hay bales . . . grain sacks," Logan said sharply, indicating the rear door. "Pile them against the wagon. Get behind them. Rose — Doc, Dinty . . . Dandy?"

"I think I'm gonna be sick," said the barber. "I thought it was all over."

"Just watch the back," Logan told them. He went up the ladder to the hayloft like a monkey, then onto the roof. The girl was flat on her stomach, looking toward the bank.

"There are too many of them left," Logan said. "It's my fault. We should've taken Maxton as he came down the street. I thought it might save some people. . . . I was wrong, dead wrong."

Then she followed Logan down into the stable.

In the hayloft she stopped him and stared into his eyes. "It ain't your fault, Logan. You tried."

"I should have known better."

"No. You tried to save the whole town. You should have known you couldn't . . . but that you had to try."

"It's no excuse," he said. "You've been a sometime girl, Dora. I want you to know I believe that."

"That's okay," she said doggedly. "Just so you don't think you're wrong."

I was wrong."

"You could've pulled out altogether," she said, on his heels to the ladder. "Just don't feel bad, Logan. I know you're goin' out there and get yourself killed. Please, just don't feel bad."

He paused a moment and managed a weak grin. "Yeah . . . you are a sometime girl," he said. Then he went sliding down to the ground floor.

Ambrose and Ed Badger stood looking out into the street. The others were huddled at the barricade so hastily erected. Sporadic shooting broke out at the rear, as Logan had expected, to demand attention there.

Ambrose drawled, "El Puma's got some Injuns in his bunch. Always has, remember?"

"They won't risk anything, now that they're together," said Logan. "There's just us three to make a real fight."

"Ha!" said Ed Badger. "We'll give 'em fight enough."

"There's maybe two dozen of them," Logan said.

"Yeah," said Ambrose. "How you reckon to make it?"

Logan shrugged. "No choice. In close."

"Yeah," said Ambrose. He had found a rifle, which he checked. "In close."

A dark-skinned Indian ran into the street from the vicinity of the bank. He held a bow and a burning arrow. A half dozen of Maxton's men and El Puma's vaqueros appeared and began laying down a steady rifle barrage. From the barn roof the Sharp's gun boomed and one of the vaqueros fell backwards.

Ambrose fired twice, but the Indian let loose the arrow. It landed perfectly on the roof.

"Time for the dance," said Logan. He waved at Dora Bell and went into the street. Ed Badger flanked him. Ambrose brought up the rear, levering the rifle. It was plain and simple suicide, Logan thought, and then he was running and ducking and firing.

They poured out of the bank to meet the challenge. The contest was completely unequal. Ed Badger's pistols flashed like leaping fish in a trout stream, Ambrose emptied the rifle and went to his two Colts, Logan was aware as they ran.

There was a clatter of sound. A buckboard with solid sides came breakneck down the street. Holding the reins in one hand, firing a shotgun with the other, was Mel Carraway. Paul Crown knelt in the body and began snapping pistol shots. As the careening wagon passed Ambrose, Crown reached down a hand. The Texan floundered aboard and Crown yelled something to the wind.

Ed Badger found shelter behind a barrel across from the bank. A shot carried away his hat and he laughed. Logan made the door to the hotel and loaded the rifle again. The enemy was a bit stunned by the accuracy of the shooting, he saw. There were several of them down. He aimed at the Indian with the bow and knocked him over. Another replaced him and Maxton and El Puma could be heard giving orders for a charge.

Mel brought the wagon swinging back down the street. Logan ran with its cover, dropping the rifle, vaulting into the body alongside Ambrose and Crown. A moment later Ed Badger swung over the tailgate and landed among them, breathing hard.

Logan said, "Nice thinkin' Mel."

"I finally seen it was my fight, too," Carraway shouted, sawing the horses to a stop in the yard of the livery.

Crown grinned. "Got us a runnin' gun wagon. Neat, ain't it?"

"Get goin' back to it," Badger complained. "They ruint my best hat." He was dexterously reloading both his guns.

"Wait a minute," said Logan. Lying on the floor of the wagon he spotted a bottle holstered under the seat. "Is that coal oil?"

"For the lantern," Mel said. "Sure, always got it."

Logan grabbed for it. There was a potato carved and shoved in the mouth for a cork. He removed it, ripped his shirt, swiftly made a tight twist into the neck of the bottle. "Something I learned from an anarchist in Chicago," he told them. "Can you get in close to the bank? They'll get your horses anyway, this trip."

"I can try," said Carraway.

"They want fire, we'll give them fire," Logan said.

Mel turned the wagon. They started down the street. Gunfire swept them, one of the horses stumbled. Carraway swung the other by main strength. Logan cupped his hands, struck a wax taper, ignited his fuse. Then he stood up in plain view and slapped the burning bomb against the wall of the bank.

There was an instant explosion. Flames soared. Yells from the enemy rent the air as Badger, Crown and Ambrose poured lead into the smoke and confusion.

Logan went down on the safe side of the wagon. The others came close behind, then fanned out as they ran for the building, peering, seeking targets. Vaqueros and Maxton's cohorts came tumbling over one another to escape the holocaust.

With only three shots left and no time to reload the Colts, Logan crouched, seeking a target which would end the conflict and send the remaining invaders or riffraff on the run. He saw Ed Badger shoot Tanner. Only the leaders were left, he thought.

He slid through a cloud of smoke into the bank building. He remembered the private office and a window at the back of the place. They would have emptied the safe by now, he knew. He ran through the door. He dove through the window into the back lot, rolling. Bullets kicked up dust about him.

He saw El Puma levelling a pistol at him and fired offhand. Then he came to one knee and there was Maxton with the derringer. He fired for the belly first, then went to the head with his last bullet.

El Puma was already dead. Maxton's low brow split open and blood poured from it. There was a carpetbag on the ground between them as they lay there.

Logan turned around. In the window of the bank building Ambrose regarded him with brooding sadness. All his suspicions returned to Logan in that instant and he knew he faced death. He threw the empty revolver at the tall Texan and tried to escape, knowing he had no chance.

Then Ambrose was turning, the gun slipping from his hand, trying to see behind him. Slowly, inexorably he slid from sight.

Ed Badger's face appeared at the opening. "Ha! You keep bad company, Daniel. That fella was about to backshoot you."

"Not quite," said Logan. "Trouble was, I held an empty hand."

He went into the building. Several of the local men were standing against a wall under guns held by Crown and Mel Carraway. There was the sound of hoofs clattering southward to inform them that the vaqueros were taking the road back to Mexico.

"Hell of a mess," said Ed Badger. "More dead people than I seen in the war."

"The town can clean it up," said Carraway. "We're just plain lucky it ain't more of us."

Logan looked at the body of Ambrose on the floor of the bank office. The fire was smoldering. Townspeople were forming a fast bucket brigade to keep it from spreading. Dinty Magin was running around in the street, his two big Germans at his side, trying to organize the effort.

Logan was suddenly dog tired and very weary. He walked down the street to the livery stable unnoticed. Pedro was there, stretched out, a bullet in his thigh, Doc Sutton working over him, Rose assisting. Mama Perdita Rugelo was reassuring her relatives.

Logan went to the black horse and began saddling up. "It's about over. Just about."

Dora Bell came close. "It's the man with the beard, like General Grant, ain't it?"

"Yes," he said.

"Can I go along?"

"No."

"Can you . . . is he . . . ?"

"I can handle him," said Logan heavily. "You wait here, Dora. I'll be back."

There were ashes in his mouth as he rode up the hill. Barty was sitting on a flat rock, wiping his eyes. Logan dismounted.

Barty said, "Got them all, huh? Got the evidence?"

"I've got it."

"Where's Ambrose?"

"Dead."

"Oh," said Barty. He stared at the ground for a long moment. "You guessed it, did you?"

"Not all the way. I knew there was something more than the drugs and the land, the dam, all that."

"But you don't know what it is?"

"Not yet."

Barty said, "I'm not going to try and gun you."

"I wish you would, Colonel. I really wish you would."

"Ambrose," said Barty with difficulty. "Ambrose was my brother."

"Your brother?" Logan was astounded.

"My younger brother. He was not very bright. Good boy, though. Loyal."

Logan said coldly, "I'm going to tell you something, Barty. He saved my life this afternoon. Then — at the end — I don't believe he wanted to kill me."

"You get him?"

"No. A friend got him. This is my town, Barty."

"Yes," said Barty heavily. "It's your town. I'll be leaving."

"If I could hang anything on you . . . but I know I can't. You're too smart for that. One thing, though. You're going to resign that government job."

"Am I?" Barty arose and moved toward his horse. "Why?"

Logan said, "Because if you don't I'm coming down to El Paso. And I'm going to shoot your brains out."

Barty considered. "Ambrose said that was

your specialty. The head shot. Yes."

"And forget trying to make that dam work for you. I'll have the money to buy you out in a day or two. You wouldn't want to own anything in this country, now, would you, Barty?"

"I'll expect to hear from your lawyer," said Barty. "I suppose you'll keep the cattle?"

"We earned it, among us," Logan said grimly.

"Yes," said Barty. "Paid for in blood. Yes. Well, I'll be seeing you, Logan."

"Not if you're lucky," Logan told him. He watched the stout, bearded man mount the sleek pony. He stayed atop the hill, his hand itching, stealing to his gun, then dropping away. Ambrose was worth two of his brother, he thought. Losing a brother like Ambrose would be the worst of it for the Colonel. He hoped he never would see the fat little brown man again, but he knew that he would.

Chapter Twelve

The last of the wetbacks were in the pasture of the Rocking Chair, eagerly nuzzling at grama grass. Pasquale and Paul Crown rode to where Ed Badger, Mel Carraway and Logan were resting from their efforts. Doc

Sutton was driving up in a carriage, Rose Maguire at his side.

"How many did you count with the scar?" Logan asked.

"About fifty," said Crown, his eyes interested, puzzled. "Should we cut 'em out?"

"Just one," said Logan.

"I don't get it," Carraway complained.

"You never do," Ed Badger commented. "Whereat's Susan today?"

"She don't feel too pretty good."

"She's mad at all of us," Badger said. "She better get over it, Mel. We're neighbors."

Mel straightened his wide shoulders, saying firmly, "I done told her. Either she gets over it, or she can go marry somebody else. I purely love her, Ed, but I mean it."

"She'll come around," Badger said. "Here, let's look at that steer."

Crown and Pasquale had the animal hogtied. Dr. Sutton came, carrying the inevitable black bag. They bent close to the prone animal and Logan pointed.

"You see that scar in the dewlap, Doc?"

"Cicatrix," said Sutton. "Healed over, that is. They have no nerves in that area." He took a sharp blade from his bag. "Interesting. Very expert stitching."

Logan said, "I remember from the dossier of Miguel de Santa Ferra, Oxford student, that he studied medicine. He was deep in Mexican politics, intrigue, you know."

Dr. Sutton arose. In his fingers he held a sparkling, shining gem. He said, "Broken from a gold mounting, see? Still traces where it had been cut and fitted."

"The crown jewels of several European countries have been missing for years," said Logan. "Fifty head, did you say, Paul?"

"Fifty," grinned the cowboy. "Maybe more."

Logan looked at the group. They waited for him to go on. He debated aloud, "How honest must we be? If we turn these over to the government with the drugs, they'll never be returned . . . for several reasons. Identification will be almost impossible. Some of the crowned heads are no longer alive or in power."

Dora Bell said, "Stop preachin' and let's put Doc to work collectin'. He and Rose want to go over to Silver and get married."

Logan said, "I think it's been proven we who are here can trust one another. Should we split the proceeds, put some of it aside for the hospital, for the Rugelos and those who saved Bailey?"

Ed Badger said, "I vote for that."

"You sure it's all right?" Carraway asked anxiously.

241

"If we keep quiet. I'm not officially with the government," Logan explained.

"Gov'ment tried to kill you, if Ambrose was gov'ment," Ed Badger said sharply. "You turned up Barty. Gov'ment owes you . . . and us, for fightin' its battle."

Logan handed the gem to Badger. "Paid for in blood. You handle it."

"Where you goin'?" demanded Badger.

"Never mind," said Logan. "Buy that land from Barty's agent, use the dam for everyone's water. Okay?"

"Well, sure. But ain't you goin' to stay?"

"Sarge should have a share, too," Logan added. He mounted the black horse. "I'll be in touch by mail."

"But we goin' to need you!"

"No, you don't need me. I'm not ready for Bailey. The blood's too fresh. Magin's too busy . . . and watch that little crook, also. I'll be riding on, now."

Dora Bell brought her horse around, smiling. The men stared at her, then at Logan. Paul Crown was grinning from ear to ear. Carraway's mouth hung open. Badger sighed resignedly.

Logan said, "Vaya con Dios, friends."

He rode out with the girl.

At the top of Mob Hill they stopped and looked back down upon the valley. She reined in close to him and was silent while he gazed.

Then he said, "Some day, maybe."

"Sure," she agreed. She patted the soft bag which held her stake. "Right now, though, let's forget it. There's Denver up high there, some place. I never seen Denver, but I hear it's full of suckers."

"It's full of sharpers, too." He tore his gaze away from the valley. 'And the Colonel will be looking for me."

She leaned toward him. "Don't be unhappy, Logan."

He kissed her. "You're some kind of a gal, all right."

"Talk western some more," she sighed. "I purely love it when you talk western."

They turned the horses north.

We hope you have enjoyed this Large Print book. Other Thorndike, Wheeler, and Chivers Press Large Print books are available at your library or directly from the publishers.

For information about current and upcoming titles, please call or write, without obligation, to:

Publisher
Thorndike Press
295 Kennedy Memorial Drive
Waterville, ME 04901
Tel. (800) 223-1244

or visit our Web site at:

www.gale.com/thorndike
www.gale.com/wheeler

OR

Chivers Large Print
published by BBC Audiobooks Ltd
St James House, The Square
Lower Bristol Road
Bath BA2 3SB
England
Tel. +44(0) 800 136919
email: bbcaudiobooks@bbc.co.uk
www.bbcaudiobooks.co.uk

All our Large Print titles are designed for easy reading, and all our books are made to last.